Trixie Dolan &
E   Sinclair

D0330998

WITHDRAWN

Shadows in Their Blood

MARIAN BABSON

Shadows in Their Blood

St. Martin's Press
New York

Library of Congress Cataloging-in-Publication Data

Babson, Marian.
Shadows in their blood / Marian Babson.
p.   cm.
"A Thomas Dunne book."
ISBN 0-312-09383-7
1. Women detectives—England—Fiction.   I. Title.
PS3552.A25S5   1993   93-22452
813'.54—dc20   93-22452   CIP

First published in Great Britain by HarperCollins Publishers.

First U.S. Edition: May 1993
10 9 8 7 6 5 4 3 2 1

Shadows in Their Blood

CHAPTER 1

The heavens had opened the day we arrived and stayed open ever since. The wind only stopped roaring long enough to draw back into itself before gusting afresh in a wild effort to smash windows and tear off roofs. Every time I looked out of the window, the rain was horizontal.

'Whitby,' Evangeline said. 'Whitby in January! My cup runneth over.'

From our sitting-room we had a great view of the ruined Abbey in the distance: a stark black silhouette against the leaden sky. Atmospheric as hell, especially with torrents of water turning the ground to mud and pouring down the slope to clog gutters and form deep pools in every hollow.

Talk about desolate! It was enough to make John Wayne burst into tears.

'It's not going to give April in Paris any competition,' I agreed.

'I shall murder Job,' Evangeline said. 'Slowly and painfully. He'll wish he'd never been born.'

A gust of wind must have hit the chimney at the right—or wrong—angle; a great cloud of smoke and cinders eddied out into the room, sending us into coughing fits. I watched a couple of live cinders hopefully. Maybe they'd set the place on fire and we could get out of here.

No such luck. One of them settled on the carpet, flared briefly and went out. Everything was too damp.

There was a long agonized scream from the street beneath our windows. Then another. And another.

'He's killing that poor girl!' Evangeline marched over to a window, threw it open, leaned out into the storm and bellowed, 'CUT!'

The sky darkened appreciably as someone switched off the lights below. For a few moments an exhausted sobbing was all that could be heard.

'God damn it! Put those lights back on!' Job's bellow was

5

even louder than Evangeline's—and more furious. 'Evangeline, shut the window and—' He reined himself in with an obvious effort. *Mind your own business* quivered in the air. 'And I'll talk to you in a few minutes,' he ended placatingly. 'Just as soon as we finish this scene.'

'He'll finish that girl first!' Evangeline drew back into the room and pulled the window shut. 'Come on, Trixie, we're going to stop him!'

'Only one more time—' we heard Job say just before the window clicked into place against a background crescendo of sobs. 'Look, I won't make you run all the way from the end of the street this time. Just from the corner, OK? OK—lights!' The sky brightened and the sobs began to fade.

We moved out into the hallway, picking our way carefully over a tangle of cables and wires. Lights dangled overhead and more wires looped in a spider's web for the unwary. We were wary; we'd been around enough film sets. Although not quite like this one.

'I've heard of living over the shop,' Evangeline complained as we stepped free of the cables and into the clear space at the top of the stairs. 'But never of living right in it. This is ridiculous!'

'It's cheap,' I said glumly. 'That's why we're stuck with it.' We might have known it would happen. We should have suspected something the instant Job telephoned us to say that we were being billeted in a four-star hotel in our own private suite. What he didn't say was that it was a defunct hotel and he had taken it over on a short-term lease so that he could shoot interiors there. A few locals had been rounded up to provide the minimum of services and to double as extras. Others in the cast had single or double rooms of their own on a descending scale of importance. Perhaps that should be ascending, as the absolute minions were living dormitory-style in the attics—and it didn't seem to be agreeing with them. The poor darlings were looking quite wan these mornings, making me wonder whether the attics were haunted—or the kids had convinced themselves that they were. It was that sort of house, a couple of ghosts

6

would come as no surprise. Whoever had named it Overlook Castle had had a great sense of humour—there was plenty that had to be overlooked.

With all the lights, the hallway was the warmest part of the building, but Evangeline was not disposed to linger. She swept down the staircase with all the imperiousness of Gloria Swanson in *Sunset Boulevard*, but she wasn't looking to her Director for instructions, she was looking to murder him.

It wasn't a bad idea, I reflected, as I followed her unenthusiastically. If something fatal happened to Job, we could give up this whole benighted project and return to London and comfort.

Something thudded against the front door just as we reached the foot of the stairs, then there was a faint scrabbling noise, as of desperate fingernails clawing at the base of the door.

'That's enough!' Evangeline declared, wrenching the door open. A wild wet gust of wind swept into our faces and moulded our skirts to our legs.

'Poor child!' Evangeline stooped to the miserable bundle of soaked rags huddled on the doorstep. 'Come inside, you're safe now—' She raised her head and glowered out into the storm at Job. 'We won't let him get at you again.'

'Can you stand up?' I crouched on the other side of the girl and tried to help Evangeline lift her to her feet. For a terrible moment I thought Job had really finished the girl. Her hair storm-plastered to her face, her make-up washed away, she looked more like a drowned corpse washed ashore from a sunken ship than an ambitious young actress willing to endure any hardship to achieve her goal. Too willing; she'd be lucky if she didn't catch pneumonia instead of stardom.

'Can you hear us?' Evangeline tugged at her arm. 'Are you conscious? Say something!'

The girl moaned faintly. She opened her mouth as though to speak, but her teeth were chattering too violently to allow her to frame any words. Her eyelids twitched as she fought to open her eyes. She moaned again and slumped back to the ground.

'Help me get her into the warmth!' Evangeline commanded, looking over her shoulder. The street outside was suddenly deserted, there was no sound except the raging of the storm. There was no one to help her but me.

Together we tugged the inert body across the threshold and into the hall. I straightened up and made an abortive attempt to close the front door, but the wind seemed to be against me, holding the door pinioned to the inside wall. It would take more strength than I had to budge it. Besides, the girl at our feet was a more immediate concern.

'Brandy!' Evangeline burrowed into one of the deep pockets of her voluminous skirt and brought out a flask. She unscrewed the cap and held the flask to the girl's white lips, tilting it slightly.

The girl gulped, choked and coughed—but it brought her back to life. Her eyes were open now, although her stare was blank. 'I—' she gasped. 'I—I—'

'It is all right, my dear.' The voice came from the top of the stairs and we all looked up automatically. Griselda von Kirstenberg stood there, smiling nastily down on us.

'You must be frightened no more,' she said to the girl. 'You have found sanctuary. You will be safe here.' She raised her head, smiling straight into a concealed camera. A muscle fluttered in her throat as her tongue tripped the tiny switch that sent her fangs sliding down into view. 'Safe . . . with us.'

Proud and sinister, she stood above us: the mother of Dracula and a vampire herself. While Evangeline and I, also vampires, but of a lesser status, crouched at the bottom of the stairs as though in obeisance.

'God damn it, Trixie!' Evangeline snarled. 'We've been set up!'

'Great! Great!' Job shouted behind us. 'Now you both smile back at her and let down your fangs while we move in for a close-up.'

'We're not wearing them,' I said. Those dental plates

8

were hideously uncomfortable and we had no intention of distorting our mouths with them until it was absolutely necessary. No one had told us we were to be in any scenes today.

'You're not?' Job was incredulous. 'But you're in full costume otherwise—'

You bet we were. Those costumes were the warmest clothes we had. When designing the costumes, Posy had specified that they must be made of the genuine merino wool so beloved of Victorians—and she was right. At fittings in London, they had seemed heavy, cumbersome and much too hot. On location up here, they were all that stood between us and hypothermia—and we blessed Posy for her forethought.

'You didn't tell us *she* was here!' Evangeline carried the battle straight into Job's own camp. She pointed accusingly at Griselda. '*No* one told us she'd arrived.'

'But everyone is arriving now,' Job protested. 'You know it's in the shooting schedule. Of course she's here and ready to work.'

'Look—' The girl at our feet had groaned again and relapsed into semi-consciousness. I abruptly changed the two cents' worth I had been about to add to the dispute. 'Look, shouldn't we get this kid to bed? And maybe get her a doctor? She looks like she's in bad shape to me.'

'She'll be all right.' Job glanced down at her dismissively. 'She's young. They can take it at that age.'

'Not if they want to reach our age.' Youth was no guarantee. The roster of young stars dimmed too early was longer than one liked to contemplate. We'd known quite a few ourselves.

'Where's Madame Defarge?' Evangeline demanded. 'What's the good of having a Stage Mother if she isn't around when you need her?'

'Defarge?' Job was momentarily baffled.

'Because she's always knitting,' I explained.

'If you mean Mrs Bright—' Job knew damned well we did. 'I think she took the bus to Scarborough for the day. Somebody gave her a ticket to the matinee of the new Alan

Ayckbourn play and when she realized all his plays pre-
miered up here and it hadn't been to London yet, there was
no holding her. She ought to be back any time now. I think
your friend Julian went with her.'

'He would!' Evangeline said. We both knew that there
would have been no holding him, either. And we had a
pretty good idea where the free ticket had come from. With
her mother out of the way, Job could work that poor girl
right into the ground with no one around to protest.

There was a slight rustle from the top of the stairs and I
looked up in time to see Griselda turn on her heel and
saunter away. The plight of a minor actress held no interest
for her. If she wasn't going to be the centre of attention,
she wasn't going to hang around.

'Oh, well—' Job waved a hand and the lights on the
landing went out. Another wave and the street outside was
noticeably murkier. In the gloom, the entrance hall seemed
to grow colder still. This wasn't helped by the rain-laden
wind still lashing in through the open door.

'I suggest you close the door,' Evangeline said icily. 'You
can't mean to do any more shooting tonight.'

'Maybe not.' Job went over and wrenched at the door.
Nothing happened. He cursed briefly, then bent and
fumbled behind it. There was a click and the door moved
easily when he straightened and tugged at it again. As it
slammed shut in the teeth of the wind, I saw two electro-
magnets had been holding it in place.

No wonder I hadn't been able to move it. King Kong
himself wouldn't have been able to budge it.

'Tell you what—' Job turned back to us with a big smile
and tried again. 'Why don't you girls run and put your
fangs in and then we'll do a couple of close-ups? Just to
round off the scene. It won't take more than a couple of
minutes.'

'No!' Evangeline said.

'No!' I agreed.

Alanna Bright moaned again, but did not open her eyes.
She was looking worse by the minute and lying there on
the cold floor was doing her no good at all.

'OK, OK!' Job gave in. He glanced down at Alanna, an expression of vague alarm crossing his face. 'She don't look so good.'

'That's what we've been trying to tell you,' I said.

'And just wait until her mother gets back and sees her,' Evangeline said with grim relish. 'Madame Defarge will have your head on a plate.'

'You wouldn't tell her?' Now Job was thoroughly alarmed.

'I won't need to. She'll notice.'

Job knew it was true. He began to lose colour slowly as he obviously pictured Mrs Bright in full cry after his head. 'I don't feel so good myself,' he said, in a feeble bid for sympathy.

'I have a splitting headache myself.' Evangeline forestalled any further self-pity. 'And—' she added pointedly, as the front door opened again and several of the technical crew swarmed into the entrance hall—'I'm frozen. Please have a light repast served to us in our rooms. Come along, Trixie.'

'Hey!' Job protested. 'What about her?' He pointed to Alanna, still sprawled at the foot of the stairs.

'That's *your* problem.' Evangeline skirted the inert form and began to ascend the stairs. 'I am *not* the Unit Medical Officer.'

That was a low blow and Job reeled from it. Everyone knew there was no Medical Officer at all with this Unit.

'Cwumbs!' A small figure detached itself from the group which had just entered. Gwenda advanced and knelt beside Alanna. 'What happened? Did she fall downstairs?'

'She never even made the stairs.' I began to feel less like a deserter; Gwenda could take over very capably. 'She's wet, frozen and exhausted. Help her to her room, will you, please?'

With a low growl, one of the men strode forward and lifted Alanna from the floor. Just before he started up the stairs, he turned to give Job a menacing glare.

'That's right.' Job shied back nervously. 'Take her

upstairs and give her a hot bath and a couple of aspirins. She'll be all right in the morning.'

'She'd better be,' the man snarled over his shoulder.

CHAPTER 2

'She's here!' Evangeline stood in the middle of the sitting-room, quivering with fury. A fresh gust of wind swirled more smoke out from the fireplace to curl around her. 'That woman is here!'

'I know,' I said. 'I saw her, too.'

'You *don't* know! And you did *not* see her!' Evangeline turned her head slowly so that her nose was pointing like a bird dog's towards the third inner door opening off the sitting-room. '*I* saw her!'

I became aware of an alien scent in the room, heavier and sweeter than the wood smoke, but just as intrusive.

'You mean she's *here?*'

'That's what I just said.' Evangeline glowered at the closed door. 'I will *not* share my suite with her! I won't have it!'

I wasn't about to turn cartwheels at the idea myself, but one of us having hysterics at a time was enough. 'Are you sure?'

'Why, no, Trixie, how could I be sure?' Evangeline lowered her voice at me, Ethel Barrymore at her most dangerous. 'It would be so easy to make a mistake about a thing like that, wouldn't it? Possibly it was just one of Job's mechanical bats flying about the room. There *is* a certain resemblance.'

'OK, OK. You know what I meant—'

'Not being a mind-reader, I fail to see how I could be expected to read anyone's mind—let alone yours.'

She paused, but I wasn't going to apologize. The wind shrieked down the chimney, sending more smoke into the room and setting us both coughing. It made Evangeline madder than ever; she hates having her Big Scenes ruined.

'So! It is you.' While we had been distracted by the smoke and coughing, the door had opened and Griselda had come into the sitting-room. 'I heard sounds and I thought perhaps they had brought the food.'

'It would choke me!' Evangeline snapped.

'Well, I'm starving and I hope they hurry up.' I had no intention of allowing Evangeline to start a cat fight. I crossed briskly to the door and looked out. It was deserted out there, but the sound of footsteps on the stairs gave me hope. 'In fact, I think someone's coming now.'

They were, but they weren't carrying trays. One of them swept a hank of dripping hair out of her eyes and grinned feebly at me as they passed. The other sketched a weary wave of the hand. They limped to the end of the corridor, paused and took deep breaths before starting up the longer, higher flight of back stairs to the upper reaches.

'Sorry, false alarm.' I backed into the room and reported. 'Just a couple of the minions going off duty for the night. I hope there's plenty of hot water for their baths. They look as though they need it.'

Griselda shrugged, dismissing anyone's problems but her own. '*I* need food,' she announced.

'We all do.' I forestalled whatever Evangeline had been about to say. I didn't trust the nasty glint in her eye. 'It should be along any minute now.'

'It will be stone cold by the time it gets here.' Evangeline was not to be placated. 'That basement kitchen is miles away.'

'We could always go down and have our meal in the canteén.' Once it had probably been a storeroom and larder adjoining the basement kitchen, but now trestle-tables and benches had transformed it into a serviceable dining-room. There were even a few round tables and proper chairs for those of us who had passed the age and stage of being willing—or even able—to clamber over benches and sit through a meal without any support for our backs.

'Don't be absurd,' Evangeline said coldly. 'I am not stirring from this suite again tonight.'

'Nor I,' Griselda said. 'I have had a long and fatiguing

journey today.' She glanced around with dissatisfaction. 'I had expected better accommodation to be awaiting me.'

'We expected better ourselves.' Evangeline matched her dissatisfaction.

'A lot better,' I agreed bitterly. 'We should have remembered that you never could trust one promise Job ever made. He's worse than a politician.'

'*Ach*, those promises!' Griselda shook her head. 'What fools we were! Where is the glamour? The luxury? Where is the surprise of my life? A shock—yes.' She glared at Evangeline. 'A surprise—no!'

'Let's face it,' I said. 'We were all suckered into this deal. Job talked about how beautiful it was in the Carpathians, about film studio facilities in Hungary, about the sidewalk cafés and boulevards of Budapest. Then when he said we'd be shooting on location, naturally we assumed that we were going to Hungary.'

'Quite right,' Evangeline said. 'There we were, all primed for goulash and gipsies, Tokay and tzigane—and what did we get? Whitby! Whitby in January!'

She had developed a nasty habit of whistling the first syllable of Whitby through her front teeth. I don't know if it bothered Job at all, but it scared the hell out of me.

'Budapest,' Griselda mourned. 'My beautiful Budapest. How I was looking forward to seeing it again!'

'You could always pay your own way,' Evangeline suggested crisply. 'It wouldn't kill you. Unfortunately.'

'*Ach*, yes!' Griselda said with malicious glee. 'You also have paid for your most recent holiday, so I hear.'

Oh dear! Bullseye!—and right on Evangeline's most sensitive spot at the moment. We just don't talk about that holiday. Not least because it wasn't at all the one Evangeline had wanted.

'And the so-happy newlyweds, they are still away?' Griselda rubbed it in for all she was worth. 'Such a charming gesture, taking the children with them.'

And that was the crux of the whole situation. Since Martha and Hugh were taking the children on honeymoon with them, Evangeline could see no reason why we

14

shouldn't go along as well. Hugh, however, could think of several reasons.

'No, no, no and no!' he had said firmly, only his sudden pallor betraying the depth of his horror at the idea.

'We'll stay at separate hotels,' Evangeline had offered nobly.

'Separate islands?' I suggested as Hugh grew even paler.

'Separate hemispheres!' Hugh had muttered under his breath. Out loud, he said, 'No, no, no and no!' again.

And so we had followed a different sun to another destination and really had quite a pleasant time after some initial difficulty. But the little American Consul on the island had been terribly sweet and assured us that he was overdue for a nervous breakdown anyway.

We might have foreseen that Job would have a fit about our tans when we got back. So vampires are supposed to be deathly pale—what is make-up for?

Grisly stood watching Evangeline with that maddening smirk on her face. How much of the story did she really know? Or was she just guessing? She knew Evangeline well enough to know her probable reaction to being left behind when there was something interesting going on.

Evangeline's eyes flashed dangerously and she had just opened her mouth with the obvious intention of annihilating Griselda when there was a tap at the door.

'The food!' I said thankfully. Tired, hungry and on edge, we desperately needed something to get our blood-sugar level back to normal. I hurried to the door and opened it. Even if the food *was* cold, I didn't care, just so long as there was plenty of it. There had been delicious savoury curry aromas wafting up from the kitchen earlier. I hoped no one had taken Evangeline's order for a light repast seriously. A lukewarm curry would still be hotter and spicier than a rapidly-cooling omelette. I really wanted a nice big plateful of curry right now.

What I got was Job. He beamed down at me, not even noticing the disappointment on my face as I looked past him, still hoping someone might be coming down the corridor bringing food. We were fed up enough with Job already.

'My darlings!' He brushed past me, strode into the room and threw out his arms expansively, then let them fall when no one rushed into them. Evangeline and Grisly regarded him with even less enthusiasm than I did.

'*Mein Liebchen*—' He concentrated on Griselda. 'I have promised you the surprise of your life—and do I deliver on my promises?'

'Not if you can help it!' Evangeline snapped.

'I do!' He ignored her. 'And here you are! Ladies, Griselda, I present to you—' he threw out one arm in a triumphal flourish—'your servant, your slave—Igor!'

I was aware of sudden movement just below my line of vision. I looked down to see a hunched misshapen figure lurch past me into the room. Half-crouching, one leg dragging uselessly behind him, back hunched, head lolling crookedly to one side, lopsided features, he made his way unerringly to Griselda and crouched looking up at her with a half-amused, half-challenging expression on his face.

It was the best make-up job I'd seen since the days of the absolute master, Lon Chaney.

'Igor!' Griselda stood motionless, looking down at him, her face frozen. She did not look as though she was having the surprise of her life. From where I stood, it looked like another shock—and a particularly nasty one at that.

Evangeline was motionless, too, a strange expression on her face as she watched them. I moved closer to her; she knew something I didn't know. I raised an eyebrow at her, but she wasn't noticing me, either. It was obviously my evening for being a non-person.

'Old friends are the best,' Job declaimed. 'Isn't it great to be reunited again after all this time? You're going to have a wonderful time working together again.'

There were definitely all sorts of undercurrents swirling around here. I edged closer to Evangeline and nudged her.

'My lady . . .' Igor moved, too. In character, grovelling, he reached out for the hem of Griselda's skirt and lifted it to kiss it.

I think he was going to kiss her hem. Griselda didn't wait to find out.

16

'There is nothing there for you any more,' she said. Her mouth twisted ruefully. 'No, nor for me, either.' She placed one foot on his shoulder and pushed him away gently.

Igor rolled with the push, doing a backward somersault and tumbling to the far side of the room.

'Wonderful! Wonderful!' Job applauded. 'We'll keep that! We'll use it! Ah, when you get creative artists together, how they spark off against each other. This picture is going to be a classic!'

Igor bounced to his feet and came up grinning. 'We were always wonderful together,' he said, more to Griselda than to Job.

'*Ja* . . .' Griselda still had a dazed look in her eyes. 'So long ago . . .'

'And so much has happened since,' Igor said mockingly. 'Do not worry. I will not try to recapture my youth. Or yours.'

Griselda flinched as though he had struck her. 'I did not mean—'

Will I ever learn? It seemed like a good idea to rush in and change the subject—whatever the subject was.

'I simply *must* congratulate you on your make-up.' Even to myself, I sounded as though I were gushing, but I had to continue. 'It's a fantastic job. You're better than Lon Cha—'

My legs abruptly went out from under me and I fell back into an armchair. Evangeline and Griselda, united for perhaps the first time in their lives, had both kicked me at the same time. I collapsed into the chair gasping. What had I done? Even Job looked embarrassed.

'Dear lady—' Only Igor was taking it calmly. 'Do not distress yourself. I am most happy that you approve of my—' He ducked his head and peered up at me. 'My . . . make-up.'

'Look.' Job took him by an elbow and began crowding him towards the door. 'Let's get out of here. We've still got a few things to talk over. I'll see you girls in the morning.'

Igor twisted to look over his shoulder at me. 'Do not

distress yourself,' he urged again. 'It is all right.' The awful thing was that he seemed to mean it.

There was a thundering silence in the room as the door closed behind them. Evangeline and Griselda stood at each side of the chair, glaring down at me. I tried to speak, but nothing came out. I took a deep breath and tried to work some moisture back into my dry mouth before I made another attempt.

'It . . . it wasn't make-up?' My voice was just a faint squeak; I prayed for them to contradict me. 'He . . . he really looks like that? All the time?'

Griselda opened her mouth, but she was having trouble speaking, too. She was in an even worse state than I was. Her own knees seemed to give way suddenly and she sank down on to the arm of my chair, shaking her head.

'He didn't always look like that.' Evangeline looked closely at both of us and wasted no time in heading for the brandy decanter. As she poured and brought the glasses to us, she continued. 'Igor Ferenczy was a Hungarian matinee idol just before the war. He was considered to be the handsomest man in Europe. Hollywood was desperate to get him and make a fortune out of him.'

'But . . .' I sipped at my brandy as Evangeline broke off and went back to the decanter to pour a glass for herself. 'What happened?'

'The Gestapo got him first.'

'*Ach, Gott!*' Griselda gulped at her brandy and choked.

'Take it easy.' I patted her on the back and caught Evangeline's hand just in time—she'd been about to sneak the opportunity to deliver a few whacking thumps. 'Why don't you just get her a drink of water instead?' I suggested.

Evangeline gave me a dirty look and moved a short distance away.

'*Nein, nein!*' Griselda gasped. 'I am all right. It is just that . . .' She closed her eyes and took a deep breath. 'I . . . I had heard. But I had not seen him before.' She dived into the brandy again; this time she didn't choke.

'We . . . vere lovers,' she said.

I nodded without surprise. I had already gathered that.

18

'He wass so young, so strong, so beautiful. It wass the last film I made before I went to Hollywood. I begged him to come with me. Everyone knew it wass just a matter of time before the Nazis took over.'

'You were making a film together?'

'*Mein Gott!*' She wiped at her eyes. 'It wass so long ago. In Budapest . . . with location shots in Transylvania. Do you believe? It wass also a Dracula film. Only then, *we* were the young lovers, the romantic leads. And now we . . . we are the *grotesques!*'

'I guess it happens to all of us eventually,' I said. 'If we live long enough.' But it wasn't much comfort.

'Igor was a hero,' Evangeline said. 'He stayed to fight the invader. He put his country first.'

'His country and his honour,' Griselda said bitterly. 'I would rather he thought of me. But no, he remained, he joined the Resistance. He was captured . . . tortured . . . ' Her eyes filled with tears, her voice wavered. 'You saw . . .'

Evangeline refilled her glass.

'He did not betray his friends.' Griselda lifted her head proudly. 'They could break his body, but not his spirit. When they realized that was impossible, they sent him to Dachau. He survived even that. He survived—but at what cost. He was so strong . . . so beautiful . . .' She took another deep gulp of the brandy.

'He survived with his spirit intact,' Evangeline said. 'Do you think he would have preferred it the other way?'

'And his friends survived—' I was feeling worse by the minute. A real hero, and I had gone and put my foot in it like that. 'The ones he refused to betray.'

'Most of them, *ja*. There were others captured who sold their comrades for their own freedom. But not Igor.' She sighed deeply. 'Igor can face himself in the mirror without loathing—despite what he sees there.'

'Well, maybe it's not as bad as it looks—' And maybe someday I'd get over this terrible compulsion to be the Little Ray of Sunshine. 'I mean, he *was* wearing some make-up. And . . . and he was really quite tall when he straightened up after that somersault. I mean, taller than he seemed when he was crawling about. I mean . . .' Oh God! it kept getting worse and Griselda was going to cry again.

'I mean, he can't be in any pain, the way he was able to fling himself around.'

'The physical pain, perhaps, has gone. But is it possible for you to imagine what he must feel otherwise? He, who had every woman sighing after him as he strolled the boulevards of Budapest, to be reduced to what his life has been since the war? A tumbler . . . an acrobat . . . in travelling circuses . . . performing throughout the Carpathians, Roumania, Transylvania . . . playing the fool . . . for the amusement of peasants . . .' Her shoulders began to heave.

The knock at the door saved us. I flew to answer it.

Some of the minions were beginning to emerge as personalities. I recognized the girl who wheeled the small hostess trolley into the room. Her name seemed to be Meta; I wasn't sure just what her job was. At the moment, she was obviously lending a hand with the catering.

'I hope you like curry,' she said earnestly. 'We could do omelettes, if you'd rather.'

'Curry is fine,' I assured her quickly. 'It smells delicious.'

'Thank you, dear, that will be delightful,' Evangeline said.

'You're sure?' She glanced doubtfully towards Griselda, who had turned her back and remained silent. 'It wouldn't be any trouble. Miss von Kirstenberg . . . ?'

'I am not hungry,' Griselda said in a muffled voice.

'It's all right.' I commandeered the hostess trolley. 'I'll take care of this, Meta.'

'I *do* have to get back to the kitchen. If you'd just leave the trolley outside your door when you're done, someone will come and collect it later.'

'We'll do that.' I urged her gently towards the door and closed it thankfully behind her.

'Apple crumble with hot custard sauce!' Evangeline had been investigating the menu. She replaced one of the lids and lifted another. 'Hmm, Brown Windsor soup to start. I suppose it will go as well as anything with curry.'

'I am not hungry.' Griselda seemed to think the

20

announcements had been made for her benefit. 'I will retire to my room. I do not wish to be disturbed.'

'We won't bother you.' I spoke quickly, before Evangeline could resume hostilities. 'You go right ahead.'

'I am sorry.' Automatically, Griselda turned and fell into her familiar pose in the doorway. 'I . . . I had not seen him before. I had heard about it, but I had not seen . . .' She made a sweeping, despairing gesture, whirled and disappeared into her room. We heard the first sobs as the door closed behind her.

'Well . . .' I turned to Evangeline. 'I guess she's human, after all.'

'And her hand is also quicker than your eye,' Evangeline said. 'You may not have noticed, but she took my brandy decanter with her.'

CHAPTER 3

As soon as the storm abated a bit, the seagulls began. They woke me in the morning with their harsh strident cries as they swooped past the windows to converge on the harbour below. The storm clouds hadn't moved very far away; they gloomed thickly on the horizon, ready, like the seagulls, to swoop down again at any moment.

It probably wasn't a wise decision to go out, but I'd been cooped up in this place for three days now and cabin fever was rapidly setting in. I dressed hurriedly—in a modern sweater and trousers for a change—and went into the sitting-room.

There was no sound from either of the other two bedrooms. The wind moaned down the chimney and sent a flurry of cold dead ashes into the room just to remind me that it was still around.

I shivered and went downstairs to the canteen, in search of human companionship as much as food—although some nice hot tea wouldn't come amiss either.

Meta was behind the long counter which had an urn of

21

coffee at one end and an urn of tea at the other. Between them, the counter was spread with fresh-baked rolls, croissants and even Danish pastries.

'Bacon and eggs?' Meta suggested as I hesitated over my choice. 'Hot toast? Kippers? Poached egg on smoked haddock? Full English breakfast? Anything you like.'

'Well . . .' I didn't want much, but she was so eager it seemed a pity to disappoint her. 'Perhaps the poached egg on smoked haddock.'

'I'll bring it over to your table,' she promised.

Gwenda waved to me from a corner table and I went over to join her. I saw why she had chosen it as soon as I sat down. It was marginally warmer there, protected by two walls from the ever-present draughts. I tucked my feet up on the rung of my chair and was almost comfortable.

'Did you sleep well?' Gwenda inquired earnestly. She did not look as though she had.

'Well enough. How about you?' She was not wearing make-up and there were dark circles under her eyes.

'I'll get used to it, I suppose.' She sighed deeply. 'But our room is wight—I mean *right*—' She was working hard to lose the twee accent she had so painstakingly acquired. 'Right under the dormitories and they're awfully noisy up there.'

'They'll quieten down when the principal filming begins.' Job would work them into exhaustion. They'd be too tired to do anything but sleep when he got through with them.

'I suppose so.' She didn't sound convinced, but she'd never worked with Job before.

'I'll guarantee it.'

'P'waps, but—'

'There you are!' Mrs Bright slammed her tray down on our table and leaned over me. 'I just want you to know that I had nothing to do with it! I think it's disgraceful!'

'Really?' She had lost me. In fact, I had never been with her, to begin with. 'Er, didn't you enjoy the matinee yesterday?'

'The matinee was fine.' She dealt the dishes from her tray to the table and sat down, dashing any hopes that she might just be passing by. She was joining us and that was

22

that. 'It was what came afterwards. I tried to stop him, but he just wouldn't listen!'

'Julian?' It was unthinkable. 'You had trouble with *Julian?*'

'He was impossible!' She added milk and sugar to her tea and stirred briskly. 'I told him it wasn't right. It showed a complete lack of respect—but I couldn't control him.'

'Julian?' It came out as a squeak. '*Our* Julian?'

'*Your* Julian.' She nodded grimly. 'I don't know that you'll be so anxious to claim him when you see what he's done. I tried to talk him out of it. Buy them a nice bunch of flowers, I told him. Get them a box of chocolates. But no—there was no reasoning with him. I just want you to know I tried my best to stop him.'

'Oh . . .' Light was dawning slowly. 'You mean he's bought us something.'

'Here you are.' Meta appeared and slid a tray in front of me.

'Mmm, that looks good.' I welcomed the opportunity to change the subject almost as much as the food. If Julian had had a momentary lapse of taste and patronized some sort of joke shop, that was between him and us. If the joke was too outrageous, Evangeline would sort him out so thoroughly that he'd never make that mistake again. If it wasn't, we might even get a laugh out of it. Mrs Bright and her opinions had no place in the matter.

'Can I get you anything else?' Meta was eager to please. 'A Danish? More tea?'

'I haven't finished this yet. No, thank you. I'm quite happy.'

She moved away reluctantly. I noticed that Gwenda watched her with narrowed eyes. She and Gwenda shared a room. I wondered if there was some friction between them. It wasn't always a good idea to lump people together as room-mates just because they were in the same age bracket.

'How's Alanna this morning?' Gwenda asked, seeming cheered by the thought that there might be a worse fate: she might have had to share a room with her mother, as Alanna was doing. 'Has she recovered yet?'

'Recovered?' Mrs Bright set down her cup and gave Gwenda her undivided attention. 'Recovered from *what?*'

23

'Oh, um, didn't she tell you?' Gwenda sent me a pleading look, but my mind had gone blank.

'Recovered from what?' Mrs Bright demanded on a rising note of hysteria. 'She just said she wanted to sleep late. What happened when I wasn't here?'

'Excuse me.' I pushed back my chair. 'This is the first halfway decent day we've had since I've been here and I want to get a breath of air.'

'What happened?' Mrs Bright couldn't have cared less about my little problems. She fixed Gwenda with a hypnotic eye. 'What hasn't my daughter told me?'

I fled.

The wind was still howling across the East Cliff as I stepped outside. One of the tourist brochures I had been reading to while away the storm-drenched hours had noted that the famous Abbey had not so much been destroyed over the years as blown away. I believed it.

It was colder than I had thought but I desperately needed air. Fresh air. I'd had enough of the smoke-choked draughts polluting our quarters. And, from the look of the storm clouds piling up on the horizon, we were going to be confined to those quarters again soon enough. I gritted my teeth and moved away from the sheltering wall of the hotel.

I had used the back door, as requested on the staff bulletin board in the canteen. The front of the house was part of the set. Job had constructed a facsimile of the cobblestoned shop-lined Church Street leading to the Church Stairs, so that the Dracula abode appeared to be on an extension of Church Street, which had mysteriously appeared at the top of the East Cliff, with the Church and ruined Abbey for neighbours. (Just why the Dracula family should be so keen about having churches nearby escaped me—unless they enjoyed dropping in now and then for a bit of desecration.)

The gravel path leading around to the front of the hotel was uneven and filled with puddles. The grass looked even wetter. I kept to the path, picking my way along carefully.

The lawn side of the hotel was opposite the West Cliff, with a splendid view of the arch made from the jawbones

24

of a whale which, from this distance, seemed to frame the statue of Captain Cook, Whitby's most famous real-life son. Behind him were the parade of successful hotels where tourists actually wished to stay. Why on earth anyone should want to build a hotel on this gale-swept bleak side of the bay was beyond my understanding.

Oh well, some people are born failures; others seem positively to work at it.

I was on the main road now and I followed the curve around to the parish church of St Mary, with its picturesque graveyard. We were scheduled to do several scenes there and I hoped the grass would have dried out by the time we got to them. Right now it was sodden and I kept to the paved pathway through the gravestones to the church and the steep Church Stairs leading down to the town. Most of the gravestones were so old and weathered that they seemed to be black-bordered; it was almost impossible to read the inscriptions on a lot of them.

I shivered—and not just because of the biting wind. People can be obliterated so quickly. A few centuries and even the faded tombstones that marked their passage were crumbling into the dust.

'That one's a pirate's grave.' Someone spoke at my side and I jumped. 'You can tell by the skull-and-crossbones. That's the way they marked them.'

'They obviously believed in calling a spade a spade in those days.' I turned slowly. My informant was the tall pale man who had carried Alanna upstairs last night.

'It all depends on how you look at it.' He shrugged. 'One country's pirate was another country's privateer. They weren't all so ill-thought of, depending . . .'

'Everything depends on your point of view,' I sighed. Especially in the film business. One company's star director was the crew's unmerciful tyrant. Which brought us back to Job.

'How is Alanna this morning?' He might have been following my train of thought.

'All right, I guess. I only talked to her mother. She said Alanna was still sleeping.'

'Best thing for her. Does Job always drive his actors like that?'

'He's notorious for it. You mean you hadn't heard?'

'Hearing's one thing. Seeing him in action is another. I never believed all I heard. Until now.'

'Job's all right, really.' I didn't sound convincing, even to myself. 'You just have to watch him.'

'Don't worry.' His voice was grim. 'I will.'

And so would Mrs Bright. I shivered again. That archetypal Stage Mother would not take kindly to the discovery that someone else had decided to look after her little girl. There were more storm clouds gathering than those over on the horizon.

'Best keep moving—' He took my arm and urged me on. 'It's too cold standing still.'

He steered me on to the path circling the church so that we approached Church Stairs by a circuitous route. We were facing into the wind now and I concentrated on fighting for breath. If it weren't for my curiosity, I would have protested, but a lifetime's experience has taught me that when a gentleman takes you the long way round it's either because he has designs on your virtue, or else there's something he wants to say. The passage of time had ruled out the first option for me, so that meant I was about to hear something I probably didn't want to know. The wind carried away my sigh.

'Breathtaking view, isn't it? he asked with a proprietorial air.

'*Something's* breathtaking,' I gasped pointedly, trying to turn away from the cutting wind.

'All that history.' He misunderstood and swung me around to face the ruined Abbey. 'You don't have things that old in America.'

'No, but sometimes I feel like it. Especially in this weather.' I tugged him back in the direction we had been heading.

'And all the legends and ghosts.' We began moving again, but at a snail's pace. 'You don't have those either.'

'Well, there's always Sleepy Hollow—'

'This very graveyard was haunted, you know. The Bargh-

26

eist Coach used to call here whenever a sailor had been buried. The night after the burial, a great coach drawn by six black horses would come galloping down Green Lane, past the Abbey and into the graveyard to stop by the new-made grave. Two outriders dressed in black carried blazing torches and the coach-driver's face was hidden by a black velvet pall. As the coach halted beside the grave, its door opened and phantom mourners, dressed in black, descended and circled the grave. On their third time around, the corpse would rise from the grave and join them. Then they all got back in the coach and the horses galloped straight down the Church Stairs. Of course, it never overturned because it was a ghost vehicle, but it came near to it . . .'

We were in sight of Church Stairs now, a long steep flight of stone steps stretching from the churchyard wall to the street a long way below. The gathering storm clouds had driven the horizon closer, the wind was even stronger, although I had not thought that possible. Around here, you didn't need to wait until night to tell ghost stories; the days were dark enough to provide the requisite spooky atmosphere. I could see why they were a popular pastime.

'At the bottom of the steps, the coach turned and raced down the street, along the lower cliff—and over the edge. Once more, the sea had reclaimed its own.'

We stood at the top of Church Stairs and looked down.

'There are one-hundred-and-ninety-nine steps.' He dropped into a more conversational tone. 'But there are several little landings where the pall-bearers used to stop and rest when they were carrying a coffin up from the town below to the graveyard. These days, they have benches on the landings, so people can sit down and rest. Of course, the churchyard isn't used for burials any more, so the Bargheist Coach never appears now.'

'I think we've gone far enough.' I stopped and drew back as he tried to lead me down the first steps. 'At least, I have. I'm not going down those steps.'

'There's a path beside them,' he offered helpfully.

'Mmm . . .' It looked worse than the steps, a breakneck descent almost straight down. I wouldn't want to attempt it without crampons and a rope. Trust Job to strand us on top of a cliff!

'It's a nice view, looking down the estuary of the Esk.' He abandoned the idea of coaxing me farther.

'It seems to be a very pretty town.' The landscape on both sides of the river was enchanting, houses and trees rising from the lower town and climbing up to the cliffs above. 'I'd like to explore it some time. When the weather's better.'

'I'll drive you down,' he promised. 'There's a much easier road, but it's much longer and it's no good for walking. There are too many bends and no pavements. It wouldn't be safe.'

'Mmm . . .' Neither steps nor path looked particularly safe to me, either. On balance, the steps were probably safer and easier—if you took your time and took advantage of the benches on the way down. But not today. A fine drenching rain was beginning to envelope us. I wondered if we would ever have a good day. 'The other cliff seems to be pretty steep, too.'

'It is.' He looked across the estuary thoughtfully. 'How would you like to be running up and down those streets with the Padfoot behind you?'

'I suppose that's another ghost legend?' He was obviously determined to give me the full treatment. I wondered whether he was trying to frighten me. And why.

'A demon in the shape of a monstrous hound—'

'Shades of the Baskervilles,' I murmured.

'Some people knew it as the barguest, or the scriker, or the gytrah, but nobody wanted to see it—or hear it. Only those who were marked for death could hear it: a howl that froze the blood and nearly stopped the heart of itself.'

'Imagine that!' He *was* trying to frighten me. He should have known that anyone who signed a contract to work with Job Farraday was not faint-hearted.

'You can scoff—'

Oh, come now. If he thought that was scoffing, wait until he heard Evangeline in action. And he would, if he tried this game with her.

'But there must be something in it. These legends crop up all over the world, in every country, in every culture.

Where did they come from, if there wasn't something there to begin with?'

It was an interesting point, but I was too frozen to stand here and argue it with him. I started to turn away.

'All right, I'll tell you a story that isn't supernatural.' Again, he mistook my reaction. I must find out what he did in the Unit; he didn't seem to be cut out for dealing with sensitive *artistes*.

'You haven't seen your Jet Shop yet.' It was a statement, not a question, but I answered it anyway.

'No, we haven't even had time to read all the script changes yet.' And there were plenty of those. Having acquired the basic script, Job was carrying on the great tradition of changing it beyond all recognition. Julian was his willing accomplice in this endeavour.

I gathered that we, as Dracula's mother and aunts, were keeping the home fires burning for him up here in Whitby, where he had landed, while he cavorted in London. The idea being that he could come up here for fresh supplies of Transylvanian earth when he required it, or, if worse came to worst, we could all sail back to Transylvania from here. In order to give ourselves something to do—and as a pretext for attracting innocent victims into our lair—we were running a jet shop. The (literally) day-to-day work was done by a local girl we had hired—and we could be found in the shop in the evenings, or the late afternoons after the sun had gone down. Since we were presumably rich and therefore licensed eccentrics, none of the locals saw anything strange in this arrangement. Rich elderly ladies were entitled to sleep as late as they wished.

'It's a beautiful shop, if I do say so myself,' he said proudly. 'There are some fantastic pieces of carving in it. You'll love it.'

'I'm sure we will.' Light was beginning to dawn in my mind, if not in the sky. 'Are you Props, then?'

'That's one name for it. Odd-job man is another. I'm Barney Pirren, the official title is Art Director, or even Production Designer. Sorry, I forgot we hadn't been introduced.'

'That's all right.' I was used to it. Half your audience

29

feels they've seen you so often that they know you person-ally. I don't mind that, but they expect it to work both ways. After all, hadn't we looked down from the screen and seen them sitting in the same seat week after week? We ought to recognize them, too. 'I'm delighted to meet you.'

His hand seemed to have a blue tinge as he extended it. I was surprised that mine didn't. What had I been thinking of to come out without gloves?

'What I was going to tell you—' He was still working towards some purpose of his own. 'Not a legend, but a local character in Victorian times. Right here, at the top of these steps, there used to be an old pedlar with a portable jet shop. There are pictures of it: a long oblong box. He could let one side down and prop the lid open to display all the jewellery and ornaments he had pinned to the lining. Fantastic. You'll love it.'

'Are you trying to tell me?' My voice sounded as danger-ous as Evangeline's in one of her Ethel Barrymore moods. 'Are you even *suggesting* that Job thinks I'm going to stand in a howling gale at the top of these stairs—?'

'No, no,' he said hastily. 'That's not what I'm trying to tell you. Besides, I'm sure Job will have one of the extras do it, if he uses the idea at all.'

'I should think so!'

'What I meant to tell you is—' He caught my hand again, his touch sending another chill down my spine. Or perhaps it was the way he looked so deeply and worriedly into my eyes.

'Don't let Job talk you into doing any stunts. Not even the simplest-seeming one. Refuse!'

CHAPTER 4

I got back to Overlook Castle one jump ahead of the deluge. The wind hurled a cascade of water at my heels as I leaped into the hall and slammed the door against it.

Evangeline had pulled a small table over to the armchair

beside the fire in our sitting-room, set her breakfast tray on it and was demolishing the last of the toast.

'Sorry, teapot's empty,' she said, as I grabbed for it. 'Where were you? You'll have to order your own.'

'I've had breakfast.' My teeth were chattering. 'I just want to warm my hands.' I wrapped them around the teapot, but they were so numb I didn't dare pick it up in case I dropped it.

'You *haven't* been outside!' Evangeline was shocked. 'Look at you! You're all wet. You must change at once—before you catch pneumonia. Although,' she added thoughtfully, 'if you *did* catch pneumonia—just a light case—perhaps we might be able to get out of here.'

'There must be an easier way to break a contract.' But she was right. Reluctantly, I forced my hands away from the comforting warmth.

'You'll want to take that along with you.' She indicated a brown paper parcel at the end of the sofa. 'It's a little present from dear Julian. Such a sweet boy.'

'Yes.' I picked it up and prodded it carefully, it was soft all the way through. 'What is it? Did you get one, too?' She didn't seem upset; in fact, she was smiling. If there was a joke, it wasn't against her.

'I most certainly did. I'm wearing mine now.'

'Wearing—?'

Evangeline gave me a saucy wink and skittishly twitched up her skirt to reveal what was still a shapely ankle. It was the same gesture with which she, as Skittles, had enraptured Edward VII in *Queen of His Heart*.

'Long Johns!' I cried rapturously. 'Thermal underwear!'

'And the matching long-sleeved undershirt.' She displayed the ribbed cuff under her black merino sleeve. 'The dear sweet thoughtful boy is a genius, Trixie. This is the first time I've been comfortable since we arrived at this benighted place. Hurry and get into yours, you'll feel so much better.'

'And that silly woman thought we'd be upset!' I was feeling better just looking at them. I hurried into my room to change, leaving the door open so that we could continue

31

talking. 'Mrs Bright tried to persuade Julian not to buy them for us. She thought it was disrespectful.'

'Julian has more sense in his little finger than she has in her whole body. The woman's an imbecile! And I'm not so sure about her daughter, either.'

'Never mind, Barney seems to like her.'

'Who's Barney.'

'He's our artistic jack-of-all-trades. You know, the Production Designer. He's designed the sets, found the props, done some of the painting and supervised the carpenters and technicians. From the way he told it, Job probably has him chopping the firewood and doing the dishes in his spare time. He's the one who carried Alanna up the stairs last night.'

'Oh yes.' Evangeline had placed him now. 'Well, I hope he isn't getting any ideas about her. There's no future there for him.'

'Why not?' He was young, charming, and would probably make a good living some day—once he broke away from Job's influence.

'Her mother has different plans for that young lady.' Evangeline's voice sharpened. 'For heaven's sake, haven't you read the gossip columns? It's been all over them for the past couple of months.'

'I've had a few other things to think about.' I kept my voice mild, trying not to imply that Evangeline might have been more helpful during our recent chaos of rescheduling a big society wedding into a discreet Registry Office affair. At least we hadn't had to send the presents back; a big society reception later, perhaps in the form of a summer garden party would take care of that. 'What have I been missing?'

'Alanna and Fabian de Bourne are the latest item. For once, her mother isn't objecting. In fact, rumour hath it that Madame Defarge did something in the Dirty Tricks line to elbow the previous American girlfriend out of the way so that Alanna could take over.'

'That doesn't sound like Stage Mothers as we know them. Except for the Dirty Tricks.' But, usually, they held on to their precious child and the tricks were used to drive away suitors.

'Ah, but there's a baronetcy waiting in the wings. Fabian is the sole heir of a rich and titled bachelor uncle who's been burning the candle at both ends for the past forty years and is now close to paying the reckoning.'

'Now I believe it.' And that meant there was trouble looming. Fabian de Bourne, playing our vampire nephew, was due to take up residence here at any moment. Barney could just forget anything he might have been thinking about Alanna. But would he?

'It's too bad, though. Barney is a much nicer person. I'm sure he'd make Alanna happier. Fabian is so . . . so . . .'

'Arrogant is the word that springs to mind.'

'Well . . . yes.' Evangeline was right. Apart from the fact that Fabian was tall, darkly broodingly handsome, and wore a cape beautifully, I'd never heard anyone say a good word about him. Except himself, of course. If he was one-tenth as good as he thought he was, we were going to create a very interesting film here. At worst, a cult film; at best, one of those box office sleepers that make *Variety* break out in banner headlines. His opinion of himself remained to be proved, but he wasn't going to take kindly to a rival.

'I have to admit it was perfect casting to get Grisly for his vampire mother,' Evangeline said. 'They both have that same arrogance. With any luck, they may begin a feud and kill each other—but not until the picture's finished.'

How many producers had said that about Evangeline herself as they pitted her against the newest egomaniacal heart-throb and stepped back out of the line of fire? She had never actually killed any of them, but she'd certainly whittled more than a few down to size.

I wasn't going to worry about it. I had towelled my feet dry and now I wriggled into fresh tights and then the long johns. Lovely! The long-sleeved shirt completed my feeling of well-being and I stretched luxuriously. *Dear* Julian, what a lovely man he was—and thank heaven he hadn't let that idiot woman talk him out of such a brilliant idea.

'Just the same—' I dived into the voluminous petticoat and skirt of my costume and surfaced again. 'It's too bad if her mother won't let Alanna choose her own husband. Barney has a much better personality—and Alanna's the one who'll be stuck with Fabian after the wedding.'

'That won't bother Mrs Bright. I suspect she has fantasies of founding a theatrical dynasty. Fabian fits into that dream much better than a mere set designer.'

'Dynasty? That's ridiculous! Those youngsters are just starting their careers. Half their reputations are sheer hype. They may both be forgotten in a few years.'

'It's all very well for you to talk, Trixie.' A snide note crept into Evangeline's voice. 'Not everyone can acquire their own theatrical dynasty ready-made, as it were.'

It was a mistake to slam the bedroom door. It let her know she had succeeded in needling me.

'Sorry.' I opened it again. 'Wind caught the door. It seems to get worse by the minute. I don't think this storm is ever going to end.'

She gave me a smug smile, letting me know that I wasn't fooling her one little bit.

'Martha has left it rather late, but I hope not too late. The stepchildren are all very well, but she ought to produce at least one child of her own. It would be a pity to let a bloodline like ours die out.'

'Martha's only one-half of any bloodline.' I kept my voice even. It was a bit late for Evangeline to be playing the Matriarch. If she'd cared that much about Martha's precious bloodline, she could have taken more of a hand in raising her.

'Oh, Hugh probably has an adequate background—we must find out more about it some day—or the children wouldn't be quite so promising. But I always say it's the bloodline through the mother that counts.'

It was the first time I'd ever heard her say that—and if she said it again, it would be the last time. I bit down on my fury, picked up my script and hurled myself into an armchair to study it.

With another smug smile, Evangeline picked up her own script and settled down.

By the time we were summoned downstairs, we both had the scheduled scene down pat. It was to take place in the jet shop when Dracula's fond aunts received the telegram from London telling them that he was weary of the social whirl—and possibly had run into a spot of trouble down there—and was about to pay them a visit. They were delighted at the prospect. An engaging young man about the house would undoubtedly attract many toothsome young maidens. Fresh blood.

We hadn't seen the set for the jet shop before. The door had been locked, perhaps because the set was still being built, or perhaps to guard against pilferage of the many tempting pieces of carved jet. You can never be too careful on the film set; some people have pretty odd ideas about what they consider to be their perks.

'How charming!' Evangeline halted just inside the door.

'Enchanting,' I agreed. Not even the bank of lights and camera equipment taking the place of the fourth wall could dispel the snug, cosy atmosphere. It was as though we had actually stepped back in time, finding ourselves in a Victorian parlour which had been transformed into a shop without losing its parlour-like appearance.

True, there were a pair of display cases crammed with carved jet jewellery and bibelots, but you would have found display cases in your typical Victorian parlour anyway. Nothing so vulgar as price tags were to be seen. Larger carved ornaments paraded across the mantelpiece: domestic animals, a lion and a unicorn, a few exotic pairs that looked as though they might once have been part of a Noah's Ark set, and, in pride of place in the exact centre, a bust of the young Queen Victoria. Several small tables were scattered around the room, tastefully littered with curios: miniature furniture (probably designed more for display than for actual dolls' houses), paper knives, inkstands with matching pens, cameos, medallions and more busts ... including one that bore a curious resemblance to

35

Griselda. I wondered if it was intentional or just a lucky find.

'Notice anything?' Barney had materialized out of the shadows behind us.

'I'm trying to notice everything,' I said truthfully. 'I'd like to be left alone here for a couple of hours, just to be able to give everything the attention it deserves.' Even the buttons on the buttonback red velvet upholstery were a gleaming black jet.

'No crosses!' Barney said triumphantly. 'Because you're vampires, see? Crosses were an important item in Victorian jewellery, but you can't have them around you. It's going to be one of the plot points by which you're eventually discovered.'

'How clever. I haven't come to that in the script yet.' In fact, because they were still working on the last half of it, but that was par for the course of any film with Job. 'You've done a wonderful job.'

'Yes, but—' He looked around with dissatisfaction. 'It should have been better. If I'd had more time. There were so many pieces I couldn't find. I've had to commission some to be made especially—and Job was furious.'

'He would be.' Anything that put the costs up would infuriate Job. He was of the Old ('A tree is a tree; shot it in Griffith Park') School.

'I'd like to be able to do more research, too.' He was still vaguely fretful. 'Jet was used as a charm against witchcraft and a protection against the evil eye. Of course, vampires aren't strictly anything to do with either witchcraft or the evil eye but . . .'

'You'd like to work it in some way.' I used my most soothing tone. It was like old times to be back stroking artistic egos.

'Exactly!' His eyes lit up, although not the way they would have done if I were thirty years younger—or Alanna. 'I was thrown into this at practically a moment's notice. And every time I tried to tell Job that I needed more time to authenticate my settings, he told me it didn't matter—nobody else would notice it.'

36

'That's Job all right.'

'Are we ready, my darlings?' Speak of the devil, here he was.

'We've been ready for ages.' I hoped I was speaking the truth. Evangeline had gone unnaturally quiet, looking down at the Griselda bust with an enigmatic expression. I crossed my fingers that she wasn't about to begin sticking pins in it. 'We've been waiting for *you*.'

'And I've been waiting for the one man we can't do without—' Job's voice was rising in that introductory way again, like a TV announcer building up to the star's entrance. 'And here he is: our principal cameraman. More, our Director of Cinematography—' He stepped to one side and we could see the small slight form which had been sheltering behind him. I blinked, then blinked again, taking in the faded Oriental features. It couldn't be! I thought he was—

'Koji!' Evangeline's delighted whoop told me it was true. 'Koji!'

'Aha, my proud beauties!' He held out his arms and we flew into them, swooping across the room like blackbirds to a nest.

'Koji, darling!' I hugged him, so delighted and relieved— and slightly guilty at thinking that he might have died. Evangeline had obviously known better. I should have kept up with the gossip more during my years in the wilderness.

'And he's still the best goddamn cameraman in the whole world!' Job proclaimed triumphantly over our heads.

'I never doubted it for an instant.' Evangeline drew back to beam into the small wrinkled face. 'My genius of light and shadow—how could you change?'

'And you, my beauty, and you.' His fingers traced her cheekbones delicately. 'You've still got those fantastic bones. That's what counts. And—' he touched the tip of my nose—'you've still got the light of mischief in your eyes. Oh, what a film we're going to make!'

We were. We were. Suddenly, we were convinced of it. We all clung to each other, threw back our heads and laughed with delight, rejuvenated. Together again, young again, with a film to make and a good time ahead.

I don't know what made me look over my shoulder. Mrs Bright was too well-padded to ever be called the skeleton at the feast, but she was sure radiating that impression. She was hugging her knitting-bag to herself and glaring at us. Strangely, along with the anger in her face there was something that curiously resembled fear.

Was she afraid that, with the Old Pals' Act so obviously in full force, her precious daughter was going to lose out when the best shots were taken?

It was more than possible that she was right. Naturally, Koji would favour old friends. He'd worked with us before, he knew our best angles, which side of our faces we preferred, how to make us look good—and he would. But that didn't mean he'd skimp on his talent with the other players. Koji was an artist to his fingertips, everyone would get the best he had to give.

'Enough! Enough!' Job shouted. 'Places, everyone. We'll have a couple of rehearsals before we start shooting. To your camera, Koji, and tell us how it looks from there.'

'Same old slave-driver,' Koji said gleefully. 'Just like old times.'

Gwenda, as shop's dogsbody and apprentice vampire, entered and dropped to her knees by the fireplace, beginning to brush at the hearthstone. Evangeline watched her and launched into the first lines of the dialogue.

I wasn't required in the scene for a few minutes, so I crossed over to speak to Mrs Bright. I figured some reassurance was required.

She took a step back as I approached and regarded me with hostility. Definitely, fences required mending here.

'I'm glad we've started at last.' I smiled at her ingratiatingly. 'It's so boring just hanging around, isn't it?'

'You gave me a nasty turn just then,' she said accusingly. 'You and Miss Sinclair. You looked like giant bats, running across the room like that. You ought to be more careful— it's dangerous.'

'Bats?' Just like her to make a comparison like that. 'You might at least have said nuns.'

'What?'

'You know—the old joke?' Her face told me that she disapproved of all jokes—old or not. 'About the drunk who found himself in court in the morning on a charge of climbing into a taxi and assaulting a pair of nuns. His defence was: "Nuns? I thought they were bats!"' Oh well, I'd known already that she wasn't going to laugh. Besides which, nuns wore modernized habits now, so the joke had lost whatever point it had once had.

'Anyway, I think that's the idea of the costume. Posy designed it that way, with batwing sleeves—' I held out my arms to demonstrate.

'Don't *do* that!' She shrank back farther.

'It's the vampire theme,' I explained. 'You know—bats, vampires, things that go bump in the night—and all that.'

'I don't like this film.' She shuddered. 'I wish I'd never let Alanna sign up for it.'

In the distance I heard Evangeline's voice rise higher as she pitched me my cue.

'Whoops! I'm on! I'll see you later.'

Stoically, she watched me cross the set. It was obviously a matter of indifference to her whether I ever spoke to her again.

CHAPTER 5

That night one of the minions had hysterics.

Not your namby-pamby shriek-and-burst-into-tears hysterics, but a full-blooded, full-throated whooping, howling hysteria that woke half the house and would have brought the neighbours running, if we'd had any neighbours nearby.

'What the devil is going on?' Evangeline appeared in my doorway.

'How should I know?' I was already groping for my robe and slippers as the unearthly screaming continued. 'It's coming from upstairs.'

'Who screams?' Griselda collided with us in the sitting-room, a black sleep mask pushed up on the top of her head like aviator's glasses.

'Upstairs,' I said grimly. 'We might as well see what it is.' As I led the way, my toe kicked something just outside the door to our suite. Automatically, I stooped and picked it up, thinking one of us must have dropped it.

'Hurry up!' Evangeline pushed me, infected by the urgency of those appalling screams. I dropped something round and knobbly into my pocket and went towards the attic stairs.

It seemed as though everyone in the house was converging on the attic. They might as well, they certainly weren't going to be able to sleep while that racket was going on.

Igor had appeared from nowhere and was crouched protectively in front of Griselda. I felt a pang of wistful nostalgia; if Martha were here, she'd be protecting me like that. Then I felt another, sharper pang. A daughter's protection wasn't the same thing at all. As I watched, trying not to be envious, Griselda reached down and tousled Igor's hair.

'OK! OK! Now what?' Job advanced upon one of the dormitory-room doors and began pounding on it. 'Shut up in there and let us in! How can anybody get any sleep around here? You're making enough noise to wake the dead—'

The screams, which had been abating slightly, took on fresh impetus. Job always was one to put his foot in it.

'Open this door!' Now he was trying to put his foot through the bottom panel of the door, kicking at it savagely.

'What is it?' Mrs Bright appeared at the top of the stairs, Alanna in her wake. 'Is someone being murdered?'

'No such luck.' Job kicked again. 'It would be quieter if she was. Come on! Open this—'

The door gave way abruptly and he lurched into the room, the rest of us crowding in behind him. Three frightened girls were huddled around the one making all the noise. The girl who had let us in scampered away from the door and rejoined them. The screamer did not notice, she seemed almost to be in a trance—a noisy trance.

'Make her stop!' Mrs Bright sounded as though she

40

might start screaming herself. 'My nerves can't take much more of this.'

'You think ours can?' Job snarled at her, then turned his attention to the minion. 'What's the matter with you? Cut that out! Right now!'

His words had no effect. My ears were beginning to hurt.

'What's the matter, honey?' Job tried a different tack. 'Tell Uncle Job . . .'

'I don't think she can even hear you,' one of the other minions said. 'She's too scared.'

'Scared? Scared? What's she got to be scared about?'

They stared at him and shook their heads wordlessly. Whatever the screamer was scared of, it was clear that the others were terrified of Job.

Beside me, Evangeline made a small explosive sound of impatience deep in her throat. I'd heard it before—when she played the Headmistress in *Scandal at Blakenfield Abbey*.

'No, wait—' I tried to stop her, but she swept past me, drawing back her hand.

The slap rang out more loudly than any scream. In the sudden silence the slapped one narrowed her eyes and turned to face this new menace, the old one forgotten.

'I'll sue you for that!' she announced. She had an American accent, not to mention frame of mind.

'Go ahead,' Evangeline said cheerfully. 'I'll probably be dead before the case gets to court—and you'll be left with all the lawyer's costs.'

That silenced the girl again—more effectively than the slap.

'That's better,' Job said. 'Now let's discuss this calmly and peacefully.'

'I'll sue you, too!' She whirled on him, but her enthusiasm drained away as she realized his chances of survival through court procedures were not much better than Evangeline's.

'Yeah, the same—with knobs on,' Job gloated. 'And I'm a sick man, too. I could pop off at any minute. So stop giving me a hard time. You don't want my heart attack on your conscience.'

41

'What about *my* attack?' She was in control now and fighting back.

'You been attacked? Who? Who attacked you?'

'Not who—what.' She raised her hand to her throat and rubbed at a small red spot. 'The bats—that's what! I've been bitten by a vampire bat!'

'Oh, nonsense!' Meta spoke from the doorway. 'There are no such things—not in Whitby. Pull yourself together, Lora. You know better than that.'

'Are you trying to tell me there are no bats in this house?' Lora faced her dangerously. 'No bats at all?'

I intercepted a swift glance from Mrs Bright. She divided it between me and Evangeline. It made me uncomfortable enough to be glad that I wasn't wearing my black costume at the moment.

'This is an old house—' Meta had begun backtracking. 'There might be a bat or two sheltering under the eaves. You can't avoid things like that in the country. But not a vampire bat—'

'Then what about this?' Lora rubbed at the red spot again. Her fingernails were long enough for her to have made it herself by stabbing her throat with them.

'Let me see that.' Job moved forward for a closer inspection. He was not impressed. 'I've seen worse scratches from a paper cut. That's just a pinprick. Hey—' He faced the others with sudden consternation. 'She's not on the needle, is she?'

'I don't do drugs!' Lora snapped.

'Yeah? Well, that looks like—'

'It was a bat! A bat, a bat, a bat—the place is full of them! Ask *her!*' Lora pointed dramatically at Meta. 'She can't deny it. She *didn't* deny it. She knows!'

'Bats won't hurt you.' Meta was looking increasingly beleaguered. 'It's all in your imagination.'

'I suppose I'm imagining the loft is full of them? We can hear them moving around up there night after night. We're all afraid to go to sleep down here in case they get in—and they did. And I'm bitten to pieces!' She clawed again at the pinprick.

42

'It's true, Mr Farraday,' one of the minions said nervously. 'There *are* bats up there. Lots of them. They frighten us.'

Evangeline made another impatient sound. I grabbed her wrist and pulled her back towards the door.

'Let's go,' I said. 'The excitement's over.'

Griselda and Igor had already turned to go. Mrs Bright was first out the door, obviously anxious to get away from all of us. We were right behind her. The drama had degenerated into a cat fight and we'd seen enough of those in our time. I just wanted to get back to bed.

As we stepped outside the door, something dark and sinister swooped the length of the hallway towards us, terrifyingly fast and menacing. Evangeline and I tried to hold our ground, but the others backed into us, shrieking and forcing us to stumble backwards into the dormitory room.

'I'm not going out there!' Mrs Bright squealed. 'She's right! There's a bat out there! My hair!' She clutched at her head, although the bat had been nowhere near her.

'It's out there?' Job brushed us aside, striding through the door. At that moment the bat caroomed away from the end wall and swooped the length of the corridor again, boxed-in and more terrified than any of us, trying to find a way out.

'Shut the door!' Lora screamed. 'Don't let it back in here!'

Griselda slammed the door hastily, leaving Job outside.

'Poor thing, you're frightening it,' Meta said.

'Let me in!' Job began hammering frantically on the door.

'Oh, for heaven's sake!' Evangeline opened the door. 'What's the matter with you? Afraid of a little bat?'

'That does it!' Job faced Meta. 'You get the exterminators here first thing in the morning. Get rid of those bats!'

'Oh yes? Yes, of course.' Meta gave a suden shrill laugh. 'Anything else you'd like done?'

He was working her too hard. He was working all of them too hard. I knew the signs. The minions had already

43

been here for several weeks doing the pre-production work. They'd be lucky if he hadn't driven them into nervous breakdowns. At best, they were preternaturally on edge.

'Just *do* it!' Job's voice was heavy with menace; he was using the veiled threat technique again. Suddenly, I couldn't stand it here a moment longer. I didn't care if the hallway, the belfry, and the whole damned place was thick with bats; I wanted out.

'Come on, Trixie!' Evangeline was having the same reaction. She never had had much patience with Job. She, too, preferred the company of bats.

Somewhat nervously, but determined, I followed her out into the hallway and down the stairs, but the bat was nowhere to be seen. He must have found somewhere to roost.

When I looked back, the others were trickling out into the hallway, cautiously looking in both directions, as though crossing a main highway, then dashing for the sanctuary of the stairwell.

Griselda and Igor were right on our heels as we got back to the suite. They held a whispered consultation in the doorway; then, somewhat reluctantly, Igor disappeared. Griselda crossed to her own room.

'I do not like this place.' She paused in her doorway and arranged herself in her familiar pose. 'These people—they are all crazy!'

I couldn't fault her on that one, but I wasn't in the mood to discuss it.

'Good night,' I said firmly.

I was taking off my robe when something fell from my pocket to the floor. I stooped and once more picked up the round knobbly object I had found on our threshold earlier. This time I looked closely at it and an icy ripple shuddered down my spine.

It was a head of garlic.

In the morning Job settled down to serious shooting, so I didn't have the time to think what I'd promised myself. It was probably just as well. Job seemed determined to keep

44

us too busy to think. I had the feeling that he had been badly shaken by last night's events.

'It's like this—' He had expounded his philosophy to me over breakfast in the canteen in the morning. It was just my luck to be right behind him in the democratic queue winding along the buffet.

'I only work with *artistes*. Genuine sensitive geniuses—' He reached out and poured himself a glass of tomato juice from the selection of jugs nestling in crushed ice.

'Umm-hmmm.' I started to follow suit until I accidentally crossed gazes with Mrs Bright. She was eyeing the jug of tomato juice with horror—as though it were chilled blood. Without a conscious decision on my part, my hand automatically swerved to the palest, most innocuous jug in the nest—either grapefruit or pineapple juice. It didn't matter which, I'd suddenly lost all appetite. Her eyes caught mine as I transferred the full glass to my tray and let me know that I wasn't fooling her for one minute—I'd *really* wanted the blood-coloured juice.

'No, you gotta make allowances—' I was his captive audience. He zoomed in on me, surrounded me, herded me towards the empty table in the corner. There was no escape. I resolved to follow Evangeline's example from now on; I'd have breakfast in the suite with her. To hell with democracy!

'Tuna fishcakes with poached egg are very good this morning,' Meta called to me as Job rushed me along the counter. 'I'll bring them to your table.'

'No temperament, no artistry, that's what I always say.' Job slammed his tray down on the table. 'A little crisis here and there? That's the price you pay for getting the best there is. It's worth it!'

'I'm sure you're right.' A lifetime of kowtowing to the Powers-That-Be had left me able to make automatic rejoinders while my own thoughts—and suspicions—continued on their uninterrupted way. 'Who *is* this Lora, anyway?'

'Brilliant!' Job said decisively. 'Brilliant! A genius in her own right!'

Can you be a genius in anybody else's right? I gave him

45

my blandest smile and tried to signal over his shoulder to Meta that I would appreciate some tea and toast. Immediately, if not sooner.

'It's my fault.' The mantle of humility sat awkwardly on Job's shoulders; he wriggled them and tried again. 'A genius is always above the common herd. I should never have suggested that she share sleeping accommodation with the kids—'

He looked deep into my eyes and I hardened my heart. There was no way I was going to volunteer the sofa in our suite. For one thing, I thought Lora was one of humanity's shabbier specimens; for another, Evangeline would kill me. And as for Griselda's reaction—

'No. No . . .' He lowered his tone to the heartfelt register he would use when trying to persuade an agent that, deeply though it pained him, for the *artiste*'s own good, he could not agree to a rise in the performance fee, nor even to equal billing with the featured players.

'No, it's my fault and I'll take the blame. Pay the price . . .' He lifted his head to stare into middle distance with an expression of ineffable dedication. 'Thoughtlessly, I demanded too much of one of Nature's more fragile and sensitive creations. I can't blame her for cracking under the strain. They live by their dreams, their imaginations—should we be surprised when those imaginations take over and prove too much for them? Lora should be with someone who can understand her and sympathize—'

I drew back involuntarily, but I needn't have worried. Job was still communing with middle distance, intent on his own preoccupations.

'I am prepared to make the sacrifice,' he announced. 'You know how I need my own space, my privacy, in order to function creatively—but so does a genius. I must bow to genius. For no one else would I do this, but . . . I am prepared to allow Lora to share my suite.'

AND ALL WAS REVEALED . . . as the subtitles to the old silent films used to shout.

I should have known it. It was a put-up job. Lora was his latest lady-friend. He'd shuffled her into the dormitory as a *pro tem.* measure and her fit of hysterics was the pretext for her transfer to his quarters. How stupid did they think the rest of us were?

'Oh, Job!' I breathed, widening my eyes. 'How kind of you. How noble!'

The only reason most of us have never won an Academy Award is that the cameras were never on us at the right moment. Some of the best acting in the world has been done off-screen.

'Yeah, well—' He swallowed it whole. 'Genius must be served . . . and all that.'

'But what exactly,' I persisted, 'does she *do?*'

'Uuuuhh . . .' That almost stopped him, but he made a relatively quick recovery. Lora is . . . is . . . a researcher. A film student. Today. But tomorrow—after she's learned her art, found her feet—'

'I see.' I batted my eyelashes at him, trying to obscure just how much I *did* see.

'Yeah. Uuhh—' He shifted uncomfortably and began searching through his pockets. 'You don't have any aspirin on you, do you? I'm getting this awful headache—'

'Sorry.' I raised my arms in a 'search me' gesture and realized again that we were being watched by Mrs Bright. And I was the one in the overgrown bat costume.

'If you ask me,' I said bitterly, 'there's too much imagination all over the place right now.'

'I'm not a hypochondriac,' he said indignantly. 'None of my ailments are psychosomatic. I'm a sick man—'

'I didn't mean you,' I said hastily, but I could see he didn't believe me. 'I was just—'

'Here you are.' Meta swooped down on us with a loaded tray and dealt out the dishes expertly.

'Thank you, but—' I recognized toast, and fishcakes with poached eggs on top, but there was a strange dark brown flat circle also on my plate. I glanced at Job's plate. He had ordered the full English breakfast and I could identify eggs, bacon, sausages, tomatoes, mushrooms and even fried bread. But he, too, had that flat brown circle on his plate.

'What on earth is that?'

47

'Try it,' Job said. 'It's delicious.' He broke off a piece with his fork and speared it.

'I didn't order anything but fishcakes and eggs,' I protested.

'Mr Farraday's orders,' Meta said. 'He wants everyone to have a piece. To sort of get you in the mood.'

'Mood for what?'

'Just try it,' Job urged. 'You'll like it.'

'I doubt it.' I looked at the dark unpleasant object—it didn't improve with closer inspection. 'And I don't think I'd like any mood that thing would get me into. What is it?'

'Black pudding,' Job said.

'Blood pudding,' Meta said at the same moment.

They stopped and looked at each other.

Blood again. The theme of this production. I didn't like it and I didn't think anyone else was going to.

'You can have my share.' I flipped it from my plate to Job's. On second thoughts, I took my plate and cup of tea and moved to an empty table. I didn't even want to look at anyone eating blood pudding.

Job was asking for trouble and I didn't want to be near him when he got it.

CHAPTER 6

I wasn't needed this morning, which left me at a loose end and roaming around to try to find a place to alight. I didn't have much luck. They were shooting Fabian's arrival, when he discovers Gwenda alone in the shop and she recognizes him as her Master, in the shop set. I drifted away, still in search of a quiet corner.

The one I found was already occupied by Griselda and Igor, deep in conversation. I didn't need the poisonous glare Griselda sent me to make me move away. I wasn't so fond of their company that I'd want to turn it into a crowd.

The erstwhile Residents' Lounge was now an impromptu

48

rehearsal studio. A troupe of the minions were choreographing their crowd scene for Fabian's progress through the town and improvising bits of business they hoped would get them noticed and perhaps earn a few extra seconds of camera time.

A promising-looking snuggery, which had originally been an alcove leading off from the pub bar, contained Mrs Bright putting Alanna through her paces. She spotted me in the doorway and frowned.

'I think Alanna should put more feeling into that line, don't you?' She appealed for my critical opinion. 'The way she's saying it right now, it sounds as though she doesn't care.'

Probably she didn't. I frowned in my turn, but not at any reading of a line. Alanna looked terrible. She was deathly pale, with large dark circles under her eyes. She turned her head listlessly to greet me and her smile was faint and forced. I'd seen healthier-looking corpses—especially those who had died during the Hollywood heyday when the Studio would send their top make-up experts to the Funeral Home to ensure that the image was sustained to the end.

'Are you all right, Alanna?' I tried to keep the alarm out of my voice. Job had probably set her on the road to pneumonia.

'Just tired, that's all.' Her smile was a trifle more natural. 'I don't seem to be sleeping too well these nights. The wind makes so much noise . . .'

'I hate this terrible place!' Uninvited, Mrs Bright weighed in with her opinion. 'It's cold and draughty, the wind never stops howling and we'll all die from secondary smoking from the chimneys alone.'

'Did you have any breakfast this morning?' I ignored Mrs Bright.

'I wasn't hungry,' Alanna said wanly.

'She's got to watch her weight, you know.' Mrs Bright spoke with the aplomb of one who never hesitated to fill her own face and quite as though her genetic bequest had nothing to do with her daughter's problem.

'You will eat lunch, won't you?'

49

'Oh yes . . .' Alanna nodded without enthusiasm. 'I know I have to keep up my strength.'

She didn't look as though she had much left. Between Job and her mother, she was being driven to the limit of her energies. I'd seen it happen before, but there isn't a great deal you can do to help the willing victims. They have to learn to fight for themselves if they're going to survive in this business. Or survive at all.

'Read that line again for Miss Dolan,' her mother urged. 'I'm sure you're not doing it right.'

'That's for Job to decide,' I said quickly. 'He's the director. Besides, I have to get back to Evangeline for our own rehearsal now.' I dodged back out of sight and hurried across the hall.

The room that passed for a library contained three book-cases, a table scattered with magazines, two armchairs and a sofa. I headed thankfully for the sofa with the feeling that I had found refuge. A loud groan from one of the armchairs shattered that illusion.

'I can't do it,' a voice said. 'I can't do it.'

'Of course you can.' I'd been around long enough to know the proper comeback to statements like that, even though I couldn't identify the voice or context.

'Do you *really* think so?' A hopeful note entered the voice.

'Of course I do.' I must have hit the right tone of absolute sincerity, for the top of a head appeared over the back of the chair and edged into view tentatively.

'But I've never done it before,' he said. 'I've only read the books. I can't really be sure it will work.' The head was covered with the soft fluffy hair that is so often a sign of early baldness, the wide startled eyes were dark amber, the small ears flattened and widened at the top, shaping into a slight point—faun's ears.

'We all have to start sometime.' Start what? I wondered. He was another perfect victim, if I'd ever seen one. Where did Job find them? 'I'm sure you'll be fine.'

'But if anything should go wrong—' He obviously required endless reassurance. 'I'd feel so awful. I'd hate to be responsible if someone got . . . seriously damaged.'

50

'Just what is it—' my own doubts deepened—'you're going to do?'

'Special effects,' he said proudly. 'It's my first time all on my own. You know—coordinating the stunts.'

'The stunts . . .' I echoed faintly. Suddenly I felt Barney's grip on my arm again, heard his insistent voice: '*Don't let them talk you into doing any stunts.*' Now I understood.

Job was planning to put our lives into the hands of this— this *faun*—who'd never done special effects before. So far as I could see, he didn't even have a back-up technical team. All he did have was a grave doubt about his own ability. A doubt I now shared. I began to wish I hadn't been so hasty in encouraging him.

'I feel so much better knowing that you believe in me, Miss Dolan.'

'I'm so glad.' I moved closer. He had been working on a coffee table in front of his chair. It was littered with sheets of paper covered with uncertain line drawings of spindly machines buttressed by mathematical equations. All too many of the equations had question-marks after them. I closed my eyes, hoping the dizzy feeling would go away.

'Maths isn't really my strong point,' he confided. He must have seen me staring at the equations. Had he registered my expression of consternation. 'But Barney says he'll check them for me.'

'Oh, fine.' But how good was Barney at maths? Not all that good, I suspected, or he wouldn't have issued his warning to me.

'Job doesn't want anything too elaborate, does he, er . . . ?'

'Oh, sorry. I'm Hobart Steele, but everybody calls me Hobie.'

'And I'm Trixie.' I returned the courtesy. 'Job doesn't want anything too elaborate . . . ?' I saw a sketch of the Church Stairs and reached for it, my blood congealing with horror. A small batlike figure was cartwheeling in the air above the stairs.

'He's got some great ideas,' Hobie said enthusiastically. 'I just hope I can live up to his confidence in me.'

I just hoped I could live. That batlike form, on closer inspection, was wearing skirts. There were no visible wires or means of support for the free-falling figure.

I remembered suddenly that no one had read the complete script. Job kept telling us that they were still writing it. After I held a council of war with Evangeline, they were damned well going to be re-writing it.

'Is anything wrong, Miss—Trixie?'

'Nothing that can't be fixed,' I said grimly. 'Do you mind if I borrow this sketch for a while?' I thought of adding that I'd bring it back safely, but had a sudden vision of Evangeline ripping it to shreds and decided I'd better not go that far out on a limb. Even the word 'borrow' was problematical.

'That's all right. Would you like any of the others?'

'Not just now, but I might come back to you later on that.' With reinforcements.

Now there was a point to wandering around the place: I had to find Evangeline and warn her about what Job was planning. And a word with Julian wouldn't come amiss. He'd been sitting in on script conferences; he might give us an idea of any other little surprises Job might have in store.

But Julian was a policeman—I might have known he wouldn't be around when I wanted him. There was no sign of Evangeline, either. I continued prowling through the public rooms of the erstwhile hotel but, although they were full of people, they were not the people I wanted to see. I was not about to go hunting through the upper floors all by myself; this benighted place was big enough to swallow up an army and still have enough room left over for a regiment or two.

The clatter of crockery drew me back to the reception area where Meta was setting out a buffet lunch on what had been the Reception Desk. It was standard lunch-time procedure for location shooting, where crew and actors could not foretell their schedules and had to grab food as and when the opportunity offered. The buffet, however, was well above standard for these occasions and I wondered again just where Job had found Meta. It was our luck that he had. I also wondered if I could get her to do the catering for Martha's belated wedding reception when the newly-weds returned.

Come to think of it, the buffet *did* look more like something prepared for a formal reception. Absently, I nibbled a devilled egg and looked at the trays of fancy sandwiches. Surely thinly-sliced brown bread, de-crusted and rolled around asparagus spears, was a little excessive for a working location lunch? And the chafing dishes filled with smoked salmon kedgeree, creamed chicken and avocado, an exotic vegetarian curry and cheese fondue, while commendable, were a bit impractical—and wait until Job saw the catering bill!

It was all delicious. I hardly realized that I had equipped myself with a plate and was helping myself to bits of everything until I bumped into Griselda, approaching with her plate from the other end of the buffet. Igor was behind her, surprisingly little on his plate, although his eyes scanned the delicacies greedily.

'Is everything all right?' Meta popped up from behind the desk, heaving a tray of fresh rolls on to the desktop.

'It's wonderful!' I said. 'I can't wait to see what you do for an encore.'

'Oh, thank you.' She blushed, she actually blushed. Either she hadn't been in this business long or compliments were rare. Frankly, it's going to be pretty experimental from now on. Mr Farraday wants me to try some Hungarian and Transylvanian recipes—to get you all deeper into the mood.'

' "*Take one cup of blood*"—' Igor's eyes gleamed unpleasantly. 'So Mr Farraday thinks inspiration lies in the stomach, like armies marching? Or is this an extension of the Method Acting I have read about?'

'I wouldn't know, but some of the recipes look very good. I'll have to go down to the town this afternoon and see if I can find the right ingredients.'

'Town?' Griselda looked up sharply. 'You are going to town this afternoon? In a car?' She looked at Igor and an unspoken message passed between them.

'You wouldn't have room for an extra passenger, would you?' I jumped in and hijacked the expedition before they could. 'I won't be needed on the set this afternoon and I'd love to do some exploring.' It was already becoming clear that if I waited until the rain stopped before I went out, I'd never go anywhere.

'We also.' Griselda glared at me. 'We would welcome the diversion of some free time away from this place.'

'Sure. There's plenty of room. The more the merrier.'

'Ve vill be sufficient, I sink.' Grisly couldn't help it; she'd played so many Nazi villainess parts, she automatically slipped into that heavy accent when she was up to no good. She didn't even know she was doing it, which was fortunate, as it helped the rest of us to keep one step ahead of her. I wondered what she was plotting now. Whatever it was, Igor was in it with her.

'I'll be leaving in about an hour,' Meta said. 'Anybody who wants to come along can meet me at the back door.'

'Going somewhere?' Lora had come up silently behind us. She was still very pale, but looked all right otherwise. Obviously, getting her own way agreed with her. 'Can I come along?'

'Sorry—' Meta radiated cold dislike. 'I'm afraid the car is full up. No places left.'

'Oh?' Lora didn't believe that for a moment. How long had she been listening? 'Maybe somebody will drop out. I'll see you at the back door in an hour. Maybe there'll turn out to be room after all.'

Don't bet on it, Lora. I decided I was on Meta's side and I'd find someone else to fill that spare seat if I had to shanghai them.

If I could get Alanna away from her mother, that would make two good deeds. I'd never seen a kid who needed a break more than Alanna; it would give her a breathing space as well as filling that extra seat.

I was sure my plans were going well when I saw Mrs Bright approaching the buffet. The coast was clear. If I hurried, I might be able to intercept Alanna before she started for the buffet and invite her to have tea in town as

54

my guest—but, how unfortunate, there wouldn't be room in the car for her mother.

Blithely planning my *coup*, it never even occurred to me to knock on the Snuggery door. (It was still one of the public rooms, wasn't it?) My mistake.

Alanna and Barney were wrapped in a clinch that would have scorched the celluloid. He must have been lurking outside waiting for her mother to disappear.

I stepped back, frantically trying to think of an explanation for my intrusion. The truth, an invitation to tea, suddenly seemed too phoney to use.

I needn't have worried. Still entwined, eyes only for each other, they turned and slipped away through a service door leading to a back corridor. I might have been invisible—thank heavens!

I waited until the door on the other side of the room closed behind them before I closed the door I was still holding open. Turning, I almost collided with Lora. I hadn't realized she had been following me. I wondered how much she had seen, but recognized glumly that little escaped those beady eyes.

'I'm sorry, Trixie.' She fixed me with a piercing gaze and advanced. 'I know you don't like me—'

'Don't be silly, dear,' I placated, backing away. 'I don't even know you.'

'That's what I mean.' She continued advancing, forcing me back. 'I think we should have a little talk.'

Abruptly, I was on the wrong side of the door and it was closing us into the Snuggery for a cosy little *tête-à-tête* I had neither wanted nor sought. I began to have some sympathy for Job; perhaps it wasn't all his fault. This was a very determined woman—and he had always been a pushover.

'I know what you must be thinking—but it's not like that at all. Really it isn't.'

'I'm sure it isn't.' It never was. 'I mean, I've not been thinking anything at all.' Except how to get out of this. I glanced over my shoulder, trying to gauge the distance to the service door. If I kept backing up slowly . . .

'I can't tell you how much I respect Job Farraday. To

me, he's like a god. Someone I'd read about all my life. I've
seen all his films over and over. I . . . I worship that man
. . . and . . . yes, I love him!'

She rather spoiled the effect of this by glancing at me out
of the corner of her eyes to see how I was taking it. With a
grain of salt, was the answer. She wasn't the first of Job's
young girls—and I very much doubted that she'd be the
last.'

'I'm sure you do,' I said soothingly.

'And he loves me. He doesn't want me to tell anyone, but
. . . we're going to be married when this filming is over.'

I was less convinced of that. Job's affections were usually
too transitory to last as far as the altar. His early life in a
community-property state had left him permanently gun-
shy. Although, now that palimony had entered the lawsuit
lists, he might consider it six of one and half a dozen of the
other.

'Don't you believe me?' Her voice rose perilously.

'Of course I do, dear.' I believe she believed it. It might
even be true. Job had a gift for getting himself into tangles
with females. I wondered if his last divorce had ever been
sorted out properly.

'You'd better,' she muttered. 'And he'd better. Anyway—' She switched on the charm again. 'We're going to be
friends now, aren't we? There's so much you can tell me
about Job in the old days. I want to hear all your stories
and—'

'Where's Alanna?' a harsh voice demanded from the doorway. Mrs Bright stood there, holding a plate of food. 'I've
brought her lunch. Where is she?'

'I don't know.' Well, I didn't. I might be able to make a
good guess, but I hadn't been asked where I *thought* she was.

'Haven't seen her,' Lora said, with a carelessness that
was more convincing than my evasion.

'I left her here.' Mrs Bright spoke as though Alanna were
an inanimate object to be set down and expected to remain
in that place. She looked around the Snuggery, frowning.

'Maybe she just slipped out to the loo,' I suggested.
'Speaking of which . . .' I made my own getaway.

56

CHAPTER 7

Meta was an excellent driver. We swooped down the long hill which was the only alternative approach to the top of the East Cliff, swung across the old bridge linking the two sides of the town, and pulled into a small car park not far from there.

'Meet me here in about two hours if you want a lift back. Otherwise,' Meta said with practised ease, 'you'll find a taxi-rank just around the corner from the railway station. Or you could find it faster and cheaper just to walk up the Church Stairs.'

'OK, thanks.' Lora was the only one young enough and tough enough to contemplate the Church Stairs without a sinking feeling. 'I might do that.' Lora was also the only one who needed to worry about expense. She turned, took a few steps sideways and seemed to vanish in a blink.

I blinked again and saw that she had disappeared into a narrow cobblestoned alleyway connecting the street with a parallel pedestrian walk.

Meta regarded the rest of us expectantly, obviously hoping we were going to vanish, too. Griselda and Igor exchanged glances, waiting for me to be the next to leave. I smiled agreeably and stood pat.

'Ve vere vondering—' Since I didn't drop dead on the spot after the killing look she sent me, Griselda gave up and got to the point. 'Could you tell us the way to a shop called *Yesterday's Dreams*?'

'Of course,' Meta said. 'But it isn't a shop. It's a new exhibition. They've got on to you already, have they? I wondered if they would.'

'That's right, I've heard from them, too.' The renewed glare from Griselda hardened my resolve. They were up to something and whither they went, I was going, too. If only out of sheer curiosity. 'I had a sweet little invitation to come and visit them. I thought I might drop in this afternoon, too.' I gave Griselda my sweetest smile. 'We can all go together.'

'Vot kind of exhibition?' Griselda asked suspiciously. I'll bet she'd attended quite a few suspect ones in her day.

'Film memorabilia,' Meta said. 'Old posters, costumes, bits of sets, furniture, props, scripts, anything to do with films from the days of the silents onwards. Actually, he really has a museum-quality collection. And he's always being wooed by museums who'd like to get their hands on it.'

'I shall never get used to being a museum piece,' I sighed.

'It is the penalty of being among the first in an industry which captured the dreams of the world,' Igor said.

'*Ja, ja!* So how do we find—' Griselda's mouth twisted ironically—'*Yesterday's Dreams?*'

'I'm afraid it's a good distance away,' Meta said apologetically. 'On top of a hill.' She looked at us and surrendered. 'Oh, all right, get back in the car. I'll run you up there.'

Up was the word. From one mountaintop to another. The Swiss and Austrians were smart enough to organize cable-cars to cover distances between peaks like this and the valleys below. The English cut more stairs.

I think we all felt a pang of apprehension as we watched Meta drive away and—so far as I could see, she did it without standing on the brake—down the minor precipice leading back to the town centre.

'We can ask them to telephone for a taxi to come and collect us when we are ready to leave,' Igor said comfortingly. He spoiled it by looking at the house and adding, 'I suppose they do have a telephone in there?'

It was a good question. The house seemed wrapped in an aura of an earlier century. It was a two-storey double-fronted building of mellow grey stone, set back from the street and surrounded by a yew hedge. Over it towered thick cypress trees, so dark a green they looked almost black.

'Ve vill get vet if ve keep standing here.' Determinedly,

58

Griselda marched down the flagstone path to the front door. There, even she hesitated.

Figures behind the lace curtains in both window bays had watched our approach but made no move to come and welcome us. It was unnerving. We stood there and looked at the motionless figures; they stood there and looked back at us, somehow exuding an air of menace. Were we intruding upon a private party? Or a coven?

'Be careful,' I said uneasily, as Igor left the path and, crouching, crept over to peek through one of the windows. I heard Griselda catch her breath.

'It is all right.' Igor straightened up, his face creased with mischief. 'They are dummies. Mannequins—in costume. Come and see.' He held out a hand to us.

'Such nonsense!' Griselda stabbed at a bell neatly centred beneath a pottery plaque which proclaimed *Yesterday's Dreams* in black Gothic lettering.

With such a build-up, the doorbell was a bit of a letdown. A perfectly demure chime sounded behind the door. After which, we had a long silence and time enough to note the water dripping from the little peaked roof overhanging the porch.

'Perhaps we should have telephoned first,' I said, then remembered Igor's doubt, which I was beginning to share. 'If they have a telephone.'

'Perhaps no one is home. Except—' Igor giggled shrilly, sounding a little mad. 'Except for the dummies.'

Griselda glanced at him impatiently. Evidently I wasn't the only one who wished he'd save his weird sound effects until he was on camera.

I felt depression settle over me. It was a long way back to town, long and steep and slippery. I wouldn't have given any great odds on all of us making it back intact.

Griselda pushed at the bell again. This time, the chimes seemed to take on an impatient note.

'Perhaps we should try the back door.' Igor giggled again and pointed to a small brass sign engraved with an arrow pointing towards a corner of the house. 'The "Tradesman's Entrance".'

'Wait.' Griselda caught him by the collar as he started for that corner. 'I think someone comes—'

There was a faint vibration beneath our feet. Given which, the least I expected was an equivalent of Man Mountain Dean to open the door. Instead, a youngish, slightish, utterly unremarkable (except for his costume) man stood there, goggling at us for a moment before he stepped back and swung the door wide.

'Come in, come in,' he said. 'What an honour. I can hardly believe—it *is* you, isn't it?' Although he directed his remarks to all of us, his eyes were fixed on Griselda.

I couldn't tear my own eyes away from *him*. He was wearing Harold Lloyd spectacles, a Laurel and Hardy bowler hat, a Douglas Fairbanks gold pirate earring in one ear (there was a faint smear of greasepaint under his other ear) and a John Wayne cowboy bandanna knotted loosely round his throat. And that was just from the neck up. I tried not to goggle, but I couldn't repress the thought that I was looking at Schizophrenia personified.

'Come in,' he urged again.

'Thank you,' Griselda said curtly, stepping into the hallway. Igor and I followed her. 'Ve haff disturbed you? Perhaps ve should come another time?'

'No! No! No!' The idea appalled him. He stretched out his hands to grasp her, then drew them back again. 'Don't think of such a thing! You're here—and welcome!'

The hallway was dark and I was uneasily aware of shadowy presences hovering behind every doorway. The man lived in a wax museum. I had the feeling that closer inspection might make me even more uneasy. There was something terribly familiar about some of those motionless forms.

'I knew you were very busy filming.' His eyes devoured us, his hands twitched again. 'I hardly dared hope you might respond to my little invitation—'

'It was very kind of you,' I said quickly, before he could get too fulsome. 'Do show us around. We're fascinated.'

'Yes, yes, of course you would be. We'll start upstairs.'

60

He began to lead the way, then stopped. 'Oh, but let me take your wraps. What must you think of me?'

I hoped he didn't really want an answer to that one. I smiled vaguely and handed him my cloak. He hung it on an old wooden rack that could have served time in the Andy Hardy series—or even *Meet Me in St Louis*.

Griselda and Igor exchanged enigmatic glances and handed him their damp coats.

'That's better.' He hung his own hat on the rack and started for the stairs again. 'Now, we'll begin at the top . . .'

Immediately behind him, as I was, I could no longer avoid noticing the rest of his outfit. It was with some relief that I saw he was wearing the ubiquitous polo neck sweater and cardigan and the sort of riding breeches favoured by certain early film directors. I had been half-afraid of encountering Tarzan's loincloth or the swaddling of Sabu, the Jungle Boy.

Not that the house was warm enough for that. We were at the very top now and the temperature gave the lie to the theory that heat rises. I shivered.

'Oh, I'm sorry.' He turned just in time to catch me. 'I'm afraid I keep the place on the cool side. It's better for the replicas, you know.'

'Yes,' I didn't know, but I was beginning to find out. As I gazed bemused at an enormous mound of artificial fruit, I realized I was looking at one of Carmen Miranda's head-dresses.

'*Mein Gott!*' Griselda gasped and I turned to find her eyeball-to-monocle with a sneering Erich von Stroheim in full Nazi uniform.

'Yes, he's rather good, isn't he?' Our host beamed. 'Even if I do say so myself.'

'They're all very good.' Dummies were carefully placed among the display cases filled with scripts and props from long-ago films. 'Do you mean to tell us you made the, er, replicas, yourself?'

'Oh yes,' he preened. 'One could never find them other-wise. I used to work at Madame Tussaud's in London. I quite liked the work, but I had to leave. I couldn't bear the way they kept replacing the models. No loyalty at all. As soon as their popularity began to fade, they'd send the figure off to be melted down and used to model some Johnny-come-lately who wouldn't last a season. Sports heroes, stage and film stars, TV characters—they all went. Only the Royal Family survived—oh, and murderers. Funny, that; murderers seem to go on for ever, while all the others fade.'

'Very funny.' I turned away, unwilling to get into a discussion on murderers. It was all very well for someone who just played with them in wax to talk, but I'd met too many in real life lately. I didn't think it was funny and I didn't want to meet them again—not even in Madame Tussaud's.

'Most amusing.' Griselda, too, had had her unwilling experience with the darker side of the world. She looked at our host with bleak disapproval.

'Oh, I didn't mean *that* kind of funny,' he said, then realized that correcting her English was not going to endear him to her either. 'I mean—Do come downstairs now. I think you'll like it better down there. I haven't quite got the arrangements the way I want them up here yet. I just wanted to give you the general idea.'

He led the way down, turned left at the foot of the stairs and switched on a light.

I gasped, Griselda purred. Igor made a strange croaking sound at the back of his throat.

We were looking into a room in which a taller, younger, larger-than-life cardboard cut-out of Griselda stood beside the fireplace while a cardboard Charles Boyer knelt at her feet.

A mannequin Griselda stood behind a red plush sofa, smiling and bending slightly, as though to catch a remark just uttered by someone sitting on the sofa—or perhaps to bestow a caress. The sofa was one of the few unoccupied spaces in the room and I got an uncanny feeling about who occupied it after the doors had been closed to the public.

'That's better.' Our host had been fiddling with the lights and now the overhead light bulb went out and a Victorian lamp glowed from a side table.

62

'I'm sorry about the light-bulb,' he apologized to Griselda, 'but it doesn't seem worthwhile getting a shade for it. I have that ceiling fixture earmarked for one of the chandeliers from *Midnight in Vienna*. I'm negotiating with a Viennese collector right now—he has three of them, but his price is too high. He wants you. I mean—' he broke off in momentary confusion. 'I mean, he wants one of my replicas of you. But I'd never part with you, my dear.'

Igor growled softly, dangerously. The hair at the nape of my neck began to prickle. I know some of the fans think they own us—but there are limits.

'Oh—forgive me!' He snapped a release catch and dropped the silken rope which barred the room. 'You must come all the way in. The room is only out of bounds to the punters. You—you're *part* of it.'

'Thank you.' Griselda stepped across the rope with queenly grace, an Elizabeth honouring Raleigh by deigning to tread on his cloak. This was her domain and she was loving every bit of it.

I was just glad that Evangeline wasn't here to see this. She didn't take kindly to having her nose put out of joint. Come to think of it, I was beginning to wish I hadn't bothered to come myself. Who needs to be a fifth wheel?

Igor must have been feeling the same way. We both hesitated beside the sofa and looked around while our host—what *was* his name? I tried to remember the improbable scrawl that had signed my invitation. Had it been a proper name or had he just signed it *Yesterday's Dreams?* I couldn't call him Mr Dreams, could I? On the other hand, it certainly suited him.

Mr Dreams led Griselda towards the cluster of dummies in the bay window. Not surprisingly, she was again prominent in the group. Igor had been watching them sardonically, now he suddenly snapped to attention and moved to join them. I followed more slowly.

The tableau in the window must have been the one that Igor glimpsed as he peered through from outside. The net curtains would have blurred his view and prevented him from distinguishing the features of the dummies. Now he stared incredulously at the young Griselda, draped in a gipsy costume still blazing with colour despite its age. Behind her was a handsome tall young man in top hat, white tie and tails. Igor winced and turned away so that his face was in the shadows.

Puzzled, I stared at the strangely-familiar male mannequin, trying to place the handsome face. Not an American actor, perhaps not English, but there was something . . .

Good Lord—it was Igor! Igor in his prime. Tall and straight, successful and happy, with his matinee idol looks and impeccable wardrobe. Oh, Igor! I winced in sympathy and tried not to look at him as he was now—or as he was then. All that remained of the young matinee idol was his fierce pride—and he must be allowed to keep that.

'*Mein Gott!*' Griselda seemed mesmerized by the tableau. I noticed that, after one swift glance, she too avoided looking at the young Igor.

'*Sorceress of Budapest,*' Mr Dreams announced proudly. 'You must remember it?'

'Could I ever forget it?' Griselda moved forward, as though in a trance. 'My last picture in Europe. Ve could hear the guns in the distance even as ve filmed the final sequences. Ve vorked vith our suitcases packed, ready to take them and run at any moment. Each night the costumes were packed in trunks, ready to load on to a lorry if ve had to make a run for it and finish the picture elsewhere. In the end, it vass so sudden . . . there vass no time. Ve left only in the clothes ve stood up in.'

Her eyes met Igor's and they were alone in the room. '*Most* of us left,' she amended.

Igor smiled sweetly. Pain clouded her eyes and she turned back quickly to the old costume, stretching out her hand and touching the heavy satin of the jacket, tracing the gold embroidery down to the braided hem, then back up the sleeve.

'So many memories,' she sighed. 'How it all comes back! But—' She snatched her hand away and peered at the sleeve unbelievingly. 'But here is the mend where I tore the sleeve in the scene running through the woods. Surely this is not the same costume? The *original* costume? From the trunk ve left behind?'

'The very same!' Mr Dreams quivered with delight at her amazement. 'Everything in my collection is the genuine article. Complete with provenance. I acquired the costume trunk from the cousin of the Wardrobe Mistress—'

'Magda!' Griselda remembered. 'That vass her name. *Ach!* She vass so cross with me for tearing my costume! She . . . survived the war?'

'Oh yes, she lived through to the 'fifties, then left her house and contents to a female cousin when she died. The costume trunk was in the attic, untouched from the day she put it there. I got a very good deal on it from the cousin when I tracked her down. Mind you, she'd no idea what she had.'

Igor shook his head dazedly and seemed to surface from some deep pool of memory. He looked at Griselda, moving his position slightly so that he did not have to look at the tableau. Griselda stared back at him; they both seemed swamped by memories.

'Incredible!' Griselda's voice might have been the voice of the mannequin, blank and colourless. 'You haff accumulated a fabulous collection, Mr . . . ' Her voice trailed off; so she hadn't been able to decipher the signature either.

'Fairbanks,' he said. 'But my friends call me Griff. My full name is Griffith Chaplin Fairbanks—I changed it by deed poll. Homage to the great, you know.'

Igor was suddenly shaken by strange choking sounds, his face contorted and he turned his head to hide it. The sudden ludicrous confession had been too much for him.

'Are you all right, sir?' Griff asked.

'My—My old war wound,' Igor choked. 'It troubles me at times.'

Griselda kicked him sharply. 'You must pay him no attention,' she told Griff. 'It embarrasses him.' But her own mouth twitched.

I was having trouble keeping a straight face myself. I longed to accuse him of blatant sexism for omitting Pickford or Swanson from the litany of great names he had assumed,

but it was obvious that he had no sense of humour at all—
or of the ridiculous.

'Oh, forgive me.' He must have sensed disenchantment
from my direction; he turned to me abruptly. 'I don't mean
to be rude. You're in the other room. This room is European
artistes. Americans are in the other room. Come this way.'
He led us across the hall to the other front room. Griselda
and Igor, still struggling for control, let me go first.

This was more like it! Or was it? For a dizzying moment,
I felt that I had stepped back in time. Old friends beamed
at me from photographs on the wall; and as for the life-size
mannequins in the bay window—

Evangeline half-turned from the window with a supercili-
ous gaze; Beauregard Sylvester, in Confederate uniform,
regarded me gravely; William Powell tapped a cigarette
against a gold cigarette case in seeming impatience and
Fred Astaire leaned nonchalantly on his walking stick.

There was a faint click behind me and a spotlight sprang
into life. Caught in its beam was a plush footstool with a
pair of dancing shoes carelessly displaying on it—*my* dancing shoes. From the distance, came the sound of an orchestra tuning up.

I was late! Automatically I started forward, reaching out
for my dancing shoes. The others were all here and in
costume. I had to get ready fast—

'Whew!' I stopped short and gave a shaky laugh. 'You
really had me going for a minute!'

'You see . . .' Griselda murmured behind me.

I saw. No wonder she and Igor had been so overwhelmed
in the other room. This place was a time-warp. An eerie
feeling swept over me that, if we didn't get out quickly, we
could be trapped here for ever.

'Yes!' Griff was delighted with my reaction. 'They *are*
your shoes. From *Dig a Bit More Gold*. I nearly got your
costume, too, but MOMI beat me to it.'

'Mommy?' Shades of Norman Bates! I looked around
nervously. Thank goodness he didn't seem to be into taxi-
dermy, but I wouldn't like to speculate what might be
underneath some of the wax coating the dummies.

'The Museum of the Moving Image,' he elucidated. 'In London, you know. They're one of my most serious competitors when the really good stuff comes up for auction now.'

'Oh yes, the Museum of the Moving Image, down by Waterloo Bridge. I've been meaning to go there.'

'My collection is better,' he sniffed. 'Smaller, but I don't have the resources behind me that they have.'

'Your collection is most impressive,' Griselda said.

'Stunning,' I agreed. I certainly felt stunned.

'But you were going to put them on.' He gestured towards the shoes. 'Please do. I'd be so thrilled.'

Luckily, he then turned to Griselda and didn't notice that I'd recoiled.

'And Miss von Kirstenberg, perhaps you would do me the honour of trying on your costume?'

'Never!' The vehemence of Griselda's reply made Griff step back. Igor tugged at her skirt, reminding her that she had a duty to be nice to her fans.

'I'm so sorry. I didn't mean to offend you.' In a moment Griff would be grovelling. 'I only thought—'

'*Nein! Nein!*' Griselda nodded at Igor and pulled her skirt away; she was in control again. 'I meant not now. Perhaps before we leave—when the filming is complete.' She gave him her most gracious smile. 'I would like to lose a few pounds first. I fear no old costume would fit me now.'

It was a great get-out line, what a pity it didn't apply to shoes. I braced myself as Griff turned back to me.

'And I must make my excuses.' Igor moved forward to save me. 'I fear I would no longer fit my costume, either.'

'Oh my God!' Griff paled as the enormity of his blunder came home to him. He stared aghast at the broken twisted body that would never again fit into the long sleek evening clothes of its youth. 'I'm sorry! I'm *so* sorry! I didn't think— I—I—' He floundered helplessly.

'I think ve must leave now,' Griselda said abruptly.

'Yes,' I chimed in, remembering my manners. 'Thank you so much for inviting us. It's been a fascinating visit.'

'I hope you'll come again.' Griff regained some of his

composure. 'And bring the others with you.' He looked at me hopefully.

'Evangeline would be delighted to come.' Ruthlessly I threw her to the wolves. Anything to get this sleigh on the road. 'I'll tell her all about it. You won't be able to keep her away.'

'Oh, good, good!' He followed us to the door where his hospitable impulse overcame him again.

'Oh, but you can't go out in that!' The rain had worsened while we had been inside and the early darkness had fallen.

'Perhaps you vould be good enough to call for a taxi?' Griselda suggested.

'No, no, I wouldn't think of it. I'll run you back myself.'

'We don't want to impose—' I tried to dissuade him, but should have known I couldn't. This was what he had been angling for when he sent us the invitation: a return entrée to the castle of his dreams.

'You'd have such a wait for a taxi. They're kept busy in weather like this. You wait here and I'll bring the car round.'

CHAPTER 8

We walked back into chaos. Even more chaos than is usual on a film location, I mean. All that was usual was that Evangeline was in the middle of it all.

We could hear the sounds of battle as we approached the front door, Griff lagging behind to admire the mocked-up street. Job was shouting with a desperate note in his voice and Evangeline was drowning him out effortlessly.

'They seem to be having a difference of opinion,' Igor remarked.

'You can say that again! No—' I stopped him as he was about to. It's always difficult to gauge a foreigner's grasp of English idiom. Igor's English was so good, if a trifle dated, that I realized I'd have to be careful. 'I mean, let's go in and see what's the matter.'

I pushed the door open cautiously. One of Hollywood's best and longest-lasting Directors had once told me: 'When you hear that note in Evangeline's voice, you approach like a prizefighter coming out of his corner against the Champ—ducking and weaving.'

I did a duck-and-weave into the front hall, with the others following behind me. They hadn't had the advantage of that conversation with the Director, but Igor was all right because of his reduced height. Griselda had her own well-honed sense of self-preservation and slid around the doorway to flatten herself against the inside wall.

Something heavy flew through the air. Job ducked and it hit Griff square in the middle of his forehead. He went down for the count.

'*Now* look what you've done!' Job roared. 'We'll all be sued!'

'*You* will be sued,' Evangeline corrected coldly.

'*Me?* It wasn't my fault. I didn't do a thing.'

'You ducked! I meant to hit *you*. It's your fault for ducking.'

'Never mind that.' I knelt on the floor beside Griff, relieved to find that he seemed to be breathing peacefully. Which was more than could be said of Job, who had begun hyperventilating.

'Did you hear her?' Job gasped. '*My* fault—'

'She is mad,' Griselda said flatly. 'Come and sit down. Do not allow her to disturb you. You must think of yourself. Of your film.'

'Yeah, you're right.' He allowed Griselda to lead him to the porter's chair in the corner. 'It wouldn't do any of us any good if I was to let her upset me into a coronary. I gotta think of the picture.'

'Try thinking about this poor man!' I snapped. 'He might have a concussion. Someone get him a glass of water.' I was loosening the bandanna around his neck. 'And send for the Unit Medical Officer.'

There was an awkward silence. I looked up to find Job busily avoiding my eyes.'

'That's right.' I remembered slowly. 'There *is* no Medical Officer on duty with this Unit.'

'It's only a few days' shoot,' Job argued. 'Maybe a couple of weeks. I figured, if anyone gets sick, we can call in a local doctor.'

This—from a man who travelled with his own pharmacopœia and wouldn't cut a fingernail without a pencillin cover!

'What do you expect?' Evangeline jeered. 'He only worries about himself, not his actors.'

'I do, too, care about—'

'Water.' Igor appeared at my side with a glass of water. Before I could stop him, he poured it down on Griff's face.

'Oh no!' I mopped at the water with the bandanna. 'What did you do that for? He was supposed to sip it.'

'It worked,' Igor said simply.

'What happened?' Spluttering, Griff began struggling to get up. 'Where am I?'

'On the floor,' Evangeline said. For the first time, she gave him her full incredulous attention, then looked at me accusingly. '*Now* what have you dragged in?' she demanded.

'Don't add insult to injury.' Job was agonized. 'He could still sue.'

'She has the luck of the devil, that one,' Griselda informed him. 'She has damaged the only person in the world who might think it an honour to be harmed by her.'

It was true. Griff was already getting his bearings and gazing upon Evangeline with adoration. Had it been possible, he would probably have amputated his goose-egg and framed it for his exhibition.

'Miss Sinclair,' he breathed. 'It *is* you!'

'Of course it is. Pull yourself together, man, and get up off that floor.'

'Evangeline—' I warned.

'Oh yes, yes, I'm sorry.' Griff floundered to his feet. 'And Mr Farraday. It's an honour to meet you, sir. I sent you a letter but—'

'Life's too short to answer letters,' Job said.

'Oh yes, yes, I understand. I agree. I wasn't complaining—'

70

'Come down to the canteen and have a cup of tea,' I invited. We wanted to keep him in a good mood.

'Stay for dinner.' Job expanded the invitation. 'What did you say your name was? We must get you to sign a release.'

'Oh yes, yes, of course.' I doubted if he knew what Job was talking about, but he'd have signed anything just to please him. Fortunately, he did not appear to be badly hurt.

'I'm Griffith Chaplin Fairbanks, by the way,' he added.

'Er, yeah.' Job rolled with the punch. 'Glad to meet you.' He threw an arm around Griff's shoulders. 'The canteen is this way.'

'All right,' I said *sotto voce* to Evangeline as we followed after them. 'What was that all about?'

'What was what about?' Evangeline's memory was short and selective. She looked at me blankly, but I wasn't buying it.

'The fight. You and Job. You threw something heavy at him. You were trying to brain him.'

'The fire tongs,' she said absently. 'But he was in no danger. He has no brain to lose.'

'Maybe. But what was it all about.'

'Oh, nothing . . .' She gave me her vaguest smile, the effect of which was nullified by the poisonous glare she directed at Job's back. His shoulders twitched, as though he had felt the needlepoint of a stiletto probing between them.

'Everything OK?' Job glanced around uneasily, perhaps to reassure himself that Evangeline was still unarmed.

'Job, dear, what could be wrong?' she asked sweetly.

'There's nothing wrong, is there?' Griff twisted round, wincing only slightly at the sudden movement. Having found us, he was in a state of terror at the thought of losing us.

'Naw, naw.' Job got a fresh hammerlock around his neck and propelled him down the stairs. 'What could be wrong? Everything's fine. Just fine.'

Several of the minions were helping Meta unload her shopping, hurrying in relays from the car to the kitchen with large cardboard boxes full of produce and staples.

71

We sat at the nearest table and Job watched with growing impatience as no one seemed to register his arrival.

'Hey!' he called out finally. 'How about some service here?'

'Just a *minute*', Meta snapped. 'Can't you see—?' She looked towards the source of the disturbance, recognizing—belatedly—Her Master's Voice.

'Sorry.' She hurried over to our table. 'Now, what would you like?'

Job looked at Evangeline and took a deep breath, restraining himself.

'Tea,' I suggested briskly. 'With all the trimmings you can muster. We've spent the afternoon at *Yesterday's Dreams*—very pleasant, but rather exhausting. We're in need of sustenance.'

'I know.' Meta regarded Griff without favour. 'These strolls down Memory Lane can be more exhausting than trying to climb Mount Everest.'

Griff flushed and looked away. She knew all right. An undefined undercurrent rippled between then and I filed the knowledge for future reference. It might be none of my business—then again, it might be.

'Hey, listen.' Job caught at Meta's arm as she moved away. 'I've got a complaint. Somebody's been nosing around in my room.'

'Oh, surely not!' She was startled. Whatever she had expected, it had not been that.

'I'm telling you. Things were all moved around when I went back after lunch. I don't like that.'

'Oh, but—' her face cleared—'the maids have to clean your rooms and make your beds. It's just standard procedure.'

'Yeah? Well, tell them they can forget it. I don't want anybody in my suite—for whatever reason. If the beds need to be made, Lora can make them.'

I glanced around involuntarily, expecting an explosion. But Lora was not in sight. Just as well. I did not have the feeling that she would take kindly to learning that her duties were going to be housewifely as well as mistressly.

'I can assure you—' Meta'a face was flushed—'the maids have more to do than worry about your business. If anyone has been "snooping" through your things, it was probably—' She broke off.

It was probably Lora. I had no difficulty in finishing her sentence in my mind. Nor did I have any doubt that she was right. Lora would not have considered it snooping; she would have been sure that she was protecting her vested interest in the man she thought was going to marry her by finding out anything there might be to know about him.

'What are you worried about?' Evangeline asked silkily. 'You're not such a fool as to carry confidential papers around with you, are you?'

Suddenly, I wasn't so sure it was Lora doing the snooping. Neither was Meta. She threw one horrified glance at Evangeline and hurried away to the safety of the kitchen.

'Never mind,' Job growled. 'So, what's your game?' He turned partial attention on Griff, while concentrating on removing a selection of pill bottles and boxes from his pockets and arranging them on the table before him.

'I don't know why you don't rattle when you walk,' Evangeline said.

'Perhaps he does,' Igor muttered. 'That is why he makes so much noise—to mask the sound.'

Fortunately, Job didn't hear him. Griff had seized the opportunity of a direct question and was embarked on a monologue about *Yesterday's Dreams*; how he got the idea, how he had amassed the collection, his hope for its future . . .

'Great, great!' Job's eyes glazed over. He began reading the small print on one of the bottles, as though hoping it might promise a cure for boredom.

'And I hope I can persuade you to contribute generously to it—'

'Huh? What?' That snapped Job back to attention. 'I dunno about that. I'm on a tight budget—usual troubles with the tax man—'

'Oh, I don't mean *money!*'

73

'You don't?' Job looked hopeful, but still wary. 'What, then?'

'Anything you can spare. Once you've finished filming, of course. Props, costumes, scripts—'

'Scripts?' Job was back on the defensive. 'I dunno—that's pretty personal.'

'Oh, I realize you'll want to have your own personal copy bound in leather and added to your collection—'

That was giving Job rather too much credit, I thought. By the time he'd finished one of his quickies, he'd forgotten he had a script. And sometimes he hadn't. A nasty suspicion began creeping up on me.

'But perhaps one of the others could spare a copy.' Griff smiled trustingly at me. Why was it always me? Did I look like the weakest link in the chain? 'Or one of the technicians. There *must* be spare scripts floating around.'

'Don't go bothering people about scripts,' Job said uneasily, as well he might. We were getting our scripts a scene at a time, shortly before shooting. None of us had seen a completed script. I doubted that there was one—

Job!' Suddenly it crystallized. 'Job, where's Julian?'

'He's all right,' Job said quickly. Too quickly.

'She didn't ask *how* he was.' Evangeline joined the battle. 'She asked *where* he was. Come to think of it, I haven't seen him all day.'

'Neither have I.' I glided over the fact that I hadn't been here all day.

'He's around.' Job didn't meet my eyes. 'You can catch up with him later.'

'He wasn't around the buffet at lunch-time,' Evangeline said thoughtfully. 'That's most unlike him.'

'Maybe he wasn't hungry,' Job said.

'That's right.' Meta appeared with the tea-tray and set it down on the table. 'I left his lunch-tray outside his door, as you instructed.' She widened her eyes, the picture of innocence, but there was meaning in her voice. 'It's still there—untouched.'

'Oh!' There was no mistaking the guilt on Job's face. 'Uh-oh!'

74

'Job! You locked him in his room!' Message received. 'How could you?'

'Be reasonable,' he said. 'It's the only way to get a script outa some of these lousy writers.'

'And not only that, you forgot to go back and unlock his door so that he could get his lunch. Oh, Job!'

'I think you forget that Julian is only a part-time writer—but he's a full-time policeman.' Evangeline's shot went home, as mine had not. Job paled.

'Very silly of you, Job.' Evangeline was delighted with the effect of her reminder. 'I'll bet he could get you on some very interesting charges. Enough to be able to lock *you* up—and throw away the key.'

'Maybe—' Job pushed back his chair—'I'd better go up and see how he's doing.'

'I'll come with you.' Job couldn't be trusted not to be side-tracked by something else on his way to Julian. He was quite capable of going off on some other project and leaving poor Julian neglected and starving in his lonely room.

'So will I,' Evangeline said.

Griselda shrugged and picked up the teapot, pouring tea for Igor and herself and—as an afterthought—for Griff.

'That's right,' Job approved. 'You act as hostess while I'm gone. Don't worry,' he added, as Griff looked anxious. 'We'll talk about this again later. You've given me some interesting ideas.'

'I'll bring up a fresh pot of tea for Mr Singer,' Meta said. 'The one outside his door will be stone cold by now.'

'Coffee,' Job corrected. 'Coffee. I want him alert—wired up.'

'But Mr Singer prefers tea.'

'Then bring him tea.' Evangeline gave Job a challenging glare.

'OK, OK,' Job said. 'Tea. I just thought—'

'I doubt that!' Evangeline turned and swept away.

'So do I!' It wasn't as good a pivot-and-sweep as Evangeline's, but it got the idea across.

Job, being thoroughly out of condition, brought up the

rear as we arrived at Julian's corridor. His door was marked by the loaded tray standing outside it.

'See?' Job said. 'I ordered him a good lunch.'

'And then took the key away with you so that he couldn't get at it! The poor boy must be starving. Julian?' Evangeline rapped on the door. 'Julian? Are you all right?'

Behind the door, the light stutter of a word-processor slowed and stopped. 'Who's there?' a voice called cautiously.

'Evangeline, dear boy!' That hadn't pleased her.

'Are you alone?' Julian was learning fast.

'I'm here, too,' I called. 'And Job—with the key.'

'Thank God!' We heard stumbling footsteps approaching. 'Open the door and let me out!'

'Not so fast,' Job said. 'You got anything for me first?'

'What?'

'How many pages have you done?'

'Oh! Oh, wait a minute—' Footsteps receded again and there was a long silence before they returned.

A piece of paper slid underneath the door, followed by another, and another . . .

'Is that all?' Job picked them up and scanned them, frowning.

'For heaven's sake!' Evangeline snatched the key away from him and inserted it in the lock. 'What do you want—blood?'

'That would do for a start,' Job agreed. 'He still hasn't quite got it. We need more gore—'

'You didn't tell me this was a splatter-film!'

'It isn't. But we're shooting in black-and-white. We need plenty of definition.'

Evangeline drew a deep breath and began to tell him what he could do with his definition, but I cut out. I was horrified to see Julian drop to his knees and launch himself at the plate of sandwiches, cramming one into his mouth despite its curling edges. He must be starving!

'Julian,' I said. 'When did he lock you in your room? When did you last eat?'

'Had dinner . . . last night . . .' His mouth full, the words

76

were indistinct, but heart-rending. 'No breakfast . . . no lunch . . . thought he'd forgotten me.'

'Would I do a thing like that?' Job asked indignantly.

'YES!' we all chorused.

'OK, OK—' He quailed before our massed fury. 'I gotta lotta things on my mind. You don't understand—'

'You locked that poor boy in *last night?*' Even Evangeline was horrified. 'He's had no food since then? That's almost eighteen hours! That's terrible!'

'Yeah.' Job frowned. 'He oughta have a lot more pages done in that time.'

'As soon as I get some strength back—' Julian reached for another sandwich—'I'm going to kill him!'

'See? I told you he was a real writer,' Job said proudly.

'I mean it!'

'You can't, Julian,' I chided. 'You're a policeman. You've sworn to uphold the law—'

'In his case, I'll make an exception.'

'Here comes Meta with some hot tea.' I spotted her at the far end of the corridor. 'That will make you feel better.'

Even as I said it, I noticed the worried look on Meta's face. But Meta always looked worried.

'Mrs Bright is looking for you,' Meta informed Job as she handed the tea-tray to Julian. 'She's right behind me— and she's on the warpath.'

'Thanks for the warning.' Job could have given Houdini lessons. He whisked the key from the lock, darted inside Julian's room, closed the door silently and locked it from the inside.

'You haven't seen me . . .' floated in the air behind him.

'Where is he?' Mrs Bright charged down the corridor, the knitting needles in her bag rattling together the way Job's teeth would if she caught up with him.

'Where is that rotten, low-down sonofabitch?'

CHAPTER 9

'Do you mean Job?' I asked innocently.

'Who else?' Evangeline raised her voice to carry through the closed door. 'The description fits him perfectly. What has he done now?'

Meta caught up the tray with the stale sandwiches and cold tea and scurried away, looking like a girl who was about to rethink her career choice. Quite a few young hopefuls did after working for Job for a while.

'Never mind!' Mrs Bright said. 'I just want to tear his head off his shoulders, that's all.'

'A worthy ambition,' Evangeline conceded. 'But can't it wait until we've finished the film?'

'It may be too late by then. My daughter's life will be in ruins!'

'Really?' That sounded a bit strong, even for Job.

'Personally, I'm in favour of a simple tar-and-feathering.' Julian raised his own voice. 'It gets one's displeasure across without being fatal. You could always kill him for an encore.'

'Is this something to do with Barney?' I tried an informed guess.

'Don't mention that name!'

Bingo! I stepped backwards as she whirled on me with a face distorted by fury.

'She thinks she wants to marry him! That man! Can you imagine? Here she's engaged to Fabian de Bourne, a lovely young man with money and almost a title, from a fine old theatrical family—and she wants to throw it all away and marry that nobody. A set designer!' She made it sound on a par with a serial killer.

'But what—' Julian was honestly bewildered—'what has Job got to do with that?'

'He hired him, didn't he? And he can fire him! I want that man off the picture! Immediately! Sent back to

78

London! Then Alanna will have time to come to her senses.'

Mrs Bright was panting slightly—of course, that might have been the stairs—and looking utterly demented. I didn't blame Job for getting out of her way. I didn't want to hang around myself.

'Well, good hunting.' Evangeline clearly felt that way, too. She took Julian's arm and moved away. 'If we see Job, we'll tell him you're looking for him.'

'That's right.' I took Julian's other arm and we dragged him away between us before he could blow the whistle on Job, which the glint in his eye betrayed that he was thinking of doing.

'I'm looking for Alanna, too,' Mrs Bright called after us.

'If we see her, we'll tell her,' I said.

For the next four days we settled down to increasingly intensive filming and I was glad that I had had my little break in town—bizarre though it had been. Heaven knew when—or if—I would ever get away from this place again.

And I had truly forgotten how boring filming could be. All those hours of waiting around while technicians made minor adjustments to the lighting, or Continuity rushed in to replace props we had moved during our scene so that the scene could be reshot, or Job went into endless huddles with Koji, Hobie, Barney and Julian, or just sat and brooded over Lord knew what. There seemed to be a thousand things that could go wrong for every one that went right. And every error was endlessly time-consuming.

Some of us read, some played cards, some gossiped, some stared into space. Madame Defarge sat there watching us all, thin steel needles flashing viciously as she worked on her everlasting knitting. I was not the only one to feel that she was spying on us—and not just keeping a hawklike eye on her daughter.

'That woman gives me the creeps!' Lora wasn't looking well. She was paler than ever and seemed thinner. She kept worrying the small scab on her neck—it would never heal

79

properly if she didn't stop picking at it. In fact, she seemed to have started a new one a couple of inches away from the first.

'She *is* pretty deadly.' I was too fed up to be discreet.

'I don't know how Alanna stands her. It's ridiculous for someone her age to have her mother riding herd on her every minute. She ought to get rid of her.'

'Easier said than done. Stage Mothers don't let go without a fight—they hang on till grim death.'

'Yeah. I guess they're like those fighting dogs that never let go—you have to club them to death before their jaws relax enough to be pried loose. I just feel sorry for Alanna.'

'I don't think you need to. She's so used to it, she probably barely notices it.' Except that she might be starting to resent that rigid control over her life now that Barney had appeared on the scene.

'I suppose she might even like it.' Lora stroked her throat thoughtfully. 'I read a story once about when Ethel Merman played that ghastly mother of Gypsy Rose Lee in *Gypsy* and after the opening some actors who'd had stage mothers of their own went backstage with tears in their eyes and told her how wonderful she was and what happy memories she'd brought back. I guess it's all in what you're used to.'

'I guess so.' I wondered what Lora's mother had been like—and what she would think about her daughter's moving in with a man three times her age in order to further her career. Maybe she'd approve. For all I knew, that was the way she had raised Lora.

'Trixie—' I didn't like the speculative glint in Lora's eye. 'Trixie, you've known Job for a long time, haven't you?'

'Umm, I'm not sure I'd say I *knew* him. I never worked with him before. The closest I came was about three sound stages away.'

'You know what I mean.' Lora shrugged away my attempt at non-involvement. 'I'm not suggesting you ever went to bed with him—'

'I should hope not!' I shuddered before remembering that she might take it personally. After all, she did.

'I mean,' she persisted, 'you were around at the same time. In Hollywood. In the old days. You must have been in a position to hear a lot of things.'

'What things?' Actually, I'd heard enough to send even a tough young modern like Lora into a fit of the vapours, but I didn't see why I should risk trouble with Job by telling her about any of it.

'*You* know—'

'Oh, Lora.' I tried reproachfulness. 'You're young and pretty—and here. Why should you care about other women in Job's past? It was long ago and in another country—' Too late I saw where this quotation was leading and broke off.

'"*And besides the wench is dead.*"' It had been too much to hope that she wouldn't recognize it. 'That's what I want to know. What killed her?'

'Who? I mean, which wench? I mean—'

'Then there was more than one!' She pounced on it instantly, her doomladen voice conveying that it was no more than she had expected.

'No! No! I mean—' I looked around frantically. How had I got trapped in this conversation? Why didn't someone rescue me?

'What were they like?' Lora wasn't going to let me escape. 'How did they die?'

Job looked across the set at us suddenly, as though suspecting he was under discussion.

'A stunt went wrong.' I lowered my voice as though he might be able to hear me. That was how they always died, working on Job's pictures. (Barney hadn't needed to worry about Job talking us into doing any stunts. We knew more than he did about Job's reputation.)

'Are you sure?' She wasn't satisfied with my answer; one hand stroked her throat again.

'That was the rumour—' Suddenly, I wasn't so sure. Why did Lora want to know? Had she a special reason? A special fear?

'LORA!' Job bellowed for her abruptly. 'Lora, come here a minute!'

81

'Why do you want to know?' I asked. 'What difference does it make?'

'Oh, no reason,' she sighed. 'No difference.' She went to obey Job's summons, leaving me with the feeling that I had failed her.

I watched Job drape a proprietorial arm across Lora's shoulders—she seemed to flinch, then brace herself—and speak to her earnestly, obviously giving her instructions, for she nodded and darted away, exuding relief.

They were about to shoot one of the key scenes and I had been on my way to watch them when Lora had intercepted me. Now I continued on my way, pausing at the edge of the set where I had a good view, but was out-of-shot. Several others had gathered there to watch, as well.

Fabian and Alanna were the centre of attention, surrounded by various minions who were brushing and tweaking at their costumes, dabbing powder on their faces, combing-out locks of hair and performing all the last-minute adjustments necessary before the camera rolls.

Evangeline stood quietly rearranging the carved jet ornaments on the mantelpiece as Gwenda twitched her skirt into more graceful folds. No one else was paying any attention to her. I knew she must be registering that fact and resenting it.

Koji approached and said something to her. It made her laugh. Well, smile. She relaxed and moved over to stand by a display case in the window. Suddenly, unnervingly, she looked just like her replica in *Yesterday's Dreams*.

I shook my head, blinked, and the resemblance vanished. Evangeline was alive and breathing, flesh and blood—but I still felt shaken.

We had all been overworking these past few days—I tried to rationalize my nervous *frisson*. Job had been living up to his reputation as a slave-driver. Even the minions, looking pale and haggard, had a tendency to jump half way out of their skins if anyone spoke to them suddenly or touched them unexpectedly. A few more days of this intensive shooting and we'd all be ready for the funny farm.

All except Job. As the saying went, he didn't have nervous breakdowns, he gave them.

'QUIET, EVERYBODY!' a minion shouted. There was silence on the set. Job strode forward and signalled. The minions melted away from Fabian and Alanna, leaving them facing each other tensely.

The only sound was the click of knitting needles going at top speed.

Job turned and glared at Mrs Bright. The sound stopped.

'LIGHTS!' Some lights dimmed, others brightened.

'CAMERA!' A clapperboard was thrust in front of the camera lens and snapped, the camera whirring.

'ACTION!' Job roared and the scene began.

They had rehearsed the scene exhaustively—perhaps more than they needed to—working together for hours, with only Mrs Bright for company, holding the script pages and taking them through the scene again and again. I suspected she was hoping that some of the latent sexuality in the scene might rekindle the flame in Alanna's heart. Barney hadn't been dismissed from the film, but he was being kept well out of the way as Mrs Bright saw to it that Fabian and Alanna were thrown together constantly.

Now, as they moved into the scene, Mrs Bright leaned forward soundlessly mouthing the dialogue with each of them in turn.

Young Dracula had come home from London for a holiday, as vampire hunters in the capital had begun to make life difficult for him. He found that his mother and aunts were saving the beautiful girl who had stumbled into their house during the storm for him. He had taken one look and been enraptured, but not in the way the elder vampires had planned.

For—and who but Job would have dared pull such a cornball routine—guess what? Down deep, Young Dracula truly yearned for the flutter of little bat wings—for an heir of his own, for the direct continuance of his own blood. And it was one of the sorrows of his existence that a lovely maiden drained of her blood was in no fit state to carry to full term and deliver a healthy child. So he must repress one almost-overpowering urge in order to indulge another and ensure his line.

This was the seduction scene—and seduction it had to be, for although he would cheerfully have perjured himself and gone through a wedding ceremony to lull his bride into a sense of security, he was most unfortunately literally unable to set foot over the doorstep of the nearby church.

His mother and aunts did not think a great deal of this newfound sensitivity and Evangeline watched with disapproval as the scene unfolded. Beyond her, on the other side of the window, was a dark shadow which was subsequently to reveal itself as the Van Helsing character, stalking Dracula with intent to end his vile practices and also, when he discovered the mother and aunts in residence, 'wipe out this vile nest of vipers'. Job was saving quite a bit of money by filming this character in shadow and silhouette; when we got back to a London studio, he'd hire the most famous name he could get cheaply, bill him as a 'cameo' and shoot a few key scenes and close-ups.

'*My dear*—' Fabian turned his melting gaze on Alanna as the scene began. '*How beautiful you are tonight. How entrancing*—' His hand crept out to hover over the long sweep of her neck rising from the low-cut gown. '*You would tempt the angels*—'

I became aware of heavy breathing behind me.

'How can she resist him?' Mrs Bright was devouring Fabian with her eyes, her bosom began to heave. 'How could any woman resist him?'

It began to look as though Fabian was going to have even more of a mother-in-law problem than I had thought.

'*Please, sire.*' Alanna dipped her head, the back of her neck was completely exposed. '*You will make me blush.*'

'*Ah yes, yes.*' He bent closer. '*The gentle suffusion of blood rising beneath that pale delicate skin*—'

'WHAT THE HELL IS GOING ON OUT THERE?' Fabian broke out of character and strode to the edge of the set, shielding his eyes to look into the gloom beyond the lights.

'I'm sorry.' Lora was back, carrying some prop. 'I

stumbled over a cable. I didn't mean to disturb you. I'm sorry.'

'CUT!' Job managed to make his bellow sound long-suffering. The lights went out on the set and up on the surrounding area. 'Now, Fabian, what's the matter?'

'Matter? Matter? Look at them!' Fabian made a sweeping gesture to encompass all of us. 'What are you doing, selling tickets? How can I work in the middle of this—this cattleyard?'

'Uh-oh,' Lora said. 'He's boiling up to it again.'

'He's so sensitive,' Mrs Bright breathed. 'Of course he can't give of his finest with all these people around.'

'Look at them all!' Fabian was working himself into a rage. 'There are dozens of people here, dozens! Get rid of them!' He pointed dramtically—unfortunately, in the wrong direction.

'Fabian, be reasonable,' Job pleaded. 'That's the camera crew. We can't get rid of *them*.'

'In the time of the Austro-Hungarian Empire,' Igor observed, 'when kings and nobles seduced the ladies, they did it with a full orchestra playing—but the musicians were blindfolded. Perhaps he would like the camera crew blindfolded—or the camera.' He gave his mad creaking laugh again and I was not the only one to wince.

'That does it!' Fabian fumed. 'Clear this set—or I walk off it!'

'Maybe that's not such a bad idea,' Job conceded. 'There *are* an awful lot of people around. OK, everybody who isn't directly concerned with this scene—off the set!'

'Oh no! And I was so looking forward to this.' I hadn't noticed Griff among the onlookers until he began moaning. 'I've never watched a film actually being shot before. Can't I just stand quietly in a corner? No one will ever know I'm here. I'll be quiet as a mouse.'

'OFF!' Job thundered. The set was not clearing quickly enough for him.

'Oh dear . . .' I thought Griff was going to burst into tears.

'Come and have some tea.' I tried to cheer him. 'You

85

can watch the next scene I do with Evangeline. Nothing puts us off our stride.'

'OFF!' Griff jumped nervously, but Job wasn't looking at him. He was glaring at Mrs Bright, who had resumed her seat and taken out her knitting. 'That means you, too!'

'Me?' Mrs Bright was incredulous. 'You can't mean me!' She looked to Fabian for support. '*I'm* part of this scene.'

Fabian turned his back on her.

'Oh!' Her gasp of outrage betrayed that this was the first time his temperament had been aimed at *her*. 'Well, if I'm not *wanted*—' She glanced hopefully at Alanna.

'Perhaps it would be better if you left, Mother.' Alanna looked nervously at Fabian, thus placing all the blame on him. 'You understand—'

'Just for this tricky scene,' Job coaxed. Something in his demeanour suggested that he was wondering how much Alanna's performance might change—and for the better— without her mother breathing down her neck.

'I suppose that means me, too,' Lora sighed, not really surprised when Job didn't bother to answer. 'You'd think one of them was going to strip off, with all this fuss about a closed set.'

'There'll be none of that!' Mrs Bright was prepared to go down fighting. 'I won't allow my daughter to be cheapened—'

'Of course not, of course not,' Job soothed. A glint appeared at the back of his eyes, then extinguished itself quickly. No, no, it wouldn't work. 'I wouldn't do a thing like that,' he said righteously.

'Please, Mother.' Alanna was close to tears.

'I'll be right outside.' Mrs Bright moved away reluctantly. 'Call me if you need me.'

'Why should she need *you?* Fabian spoke over his shoulder dismissively. '*I'm* going to be looking after her from now on.'

Mrs Bright froze. For the first time, perhaps, she seemed to realize that her daughter's marriage might not be the idyllic *ménage à trois* she had been envisioning. Something dangerous flashed in her eyes. I got the feeling that the odds against Barney had suddenly changed.

'I'm not actually involved in this scene.' It was most unlike Evangeline to act as peace-maker. 'I'll leave the set, too. You can always cut in my reactions when we reach the editing stage.'

'Great! Great!' Job was so relieved at the unexpected cooperation that he forgot to be suspicious of it. 'Wonderful idea, sweetheart. You go and get your tea. Everybody go get your tea.'

'I'll be in our room,' Mrs Bright announced to her daughter, 'when you need *me*.' She went off in the opposite direction to the rest of us.

'This is just the start—' Clinging to the banister as we went downstairs, Lora seemed to be muttering to herself. Or perhaps to anyone who wanted to listen.

'What did you say, dear?' I was beginning to worry about her. She was too pale and wan; she clung to the banister tightly, like a much older person afraid of stumbling. In an earlier age, people might have said there was something preying on her mind. In her present circumstances, dancing attendance on Job day *and* night, I feared only the word 'preying' applied. Job had always been notorious for draining the energies and talents of those foolish enough to get too close to him—and of discarding them ruthlessly when they could no longer keep up with his demands.

'Starting again—' Lora nearly tripped and I caught her arm.

'What's starting, dear?' Instantly, I regretted my question, hoping she wouldn't bellow out the answer. She looked unhealthy enough for it to be some fatal wasting disease, but it was probably something more prosaic and I didn't really want to know. It's all very well for people these days to talk about how much better it is to discuss everything openly and at exhaustive length, but I mourn the loss of a bit of decent reticence.

'*He* is. He's going to do it again. He does it on almost every film—he's got a reputation for it. I tried to warn Job, but he just laughed and told me not to worry.'

87

Well that cleared up the *He*. The next question was 'Worry about what?'

'Fabian ruining the picture.' I was thankful that we had reached the foot of the stairs safely and now Lora paused. Igor and Griff, leading the group of displaced extras and technicians, went ahead into the canteen, but Evangeline noticed that we were lagging behind and came back to see what she was missing.

'He won't ruin the picture, he's not that bad an actor,' Evangeline said. 'He's not as good as he thinks he is, but he isn't carrying the picture alone. The rest of us can cover for him if he makes mistakes.'

'No, it's not that.' Lora faced us earnestly, tragically, to impart the awful secret. 'He . . . he walks out. He's been doing it on all his pictures lately, that's why Job was able to get him so cheaply. Word is getting around, although the public doesn't know it yet.'

'Walks out?' Evangeline looked at her blankly.

'He waits until the picture is well under way, when half the important scenes are in the can, but there are several key scenes still to be shot, then he walks out . . . runs away . . . and sends word that he won't come back until he gets a lot more money. And they have to pay him because, if they don't, he won't come back and they've got no picture.' Her voice fell, her tragic eyes shared with us the enormity of it.

'Is that all?' Evangeline and I looked at each other and horrified poor Lora by bursting into laughter.

'Dear God, I'd forgotten they could still be so wet behind the ears!' Evangeline whooped.

'Don't look so shocked, Lora.' I struggled for composure. 'That trick is as old as the movie business itself. Some of the biggest names in Silents had it down to a fine art.'

'And usually the money went straight to their cocaine dealers.' Evangeline was sobering. 'That wasn't so funny. But that isn't new, either.'

'There's nothing new under the sun,' I agreed. 'You don't have to worry about Job, Lora, he cut his teeth on people like that. He'll eat Fabian for breakfast if he tries that trick.'

'Do you remember the time Beaure—' Evangeline began, but I interrupted her. Lora had begun swaying and I was afraid she was going to faint.

'Lora, I think you need rest more than you need tea. Why don't you go up and lie down? Get some sleep while Job is busy—' Whoops! That wasn't tactful, but Lora didn't appear to notice.

'I think maybe I will.' She gave us a wan smile. 'I'm not feeling so well these days. I'll be glad when we move back to London.'

CHAPTER 10

There was a pungent odour in the lower hallway, growing stronger the nearer we got to the kitchen adjoining the canteen.

'I don't know about you,' Evangeline said, 'but I'm getting very bored with garlic.'

'I've had enough to last me the rest of my life,' I agreed. True, I hadn't found any more strewn in front of our doorway, but that was probably because it was all going into the cooking. Any day now, I expected to find a few cloves of the stuff bobbing amongst the tealeaves in the teapot.

'And what—' Evangeline lifted her head and sniffed the air mistrustingly—'*what* are they mixing it with this time?'

'Something fishy?' I sniffed, too, but couldn't identify the base scent. We exchanged glances.

'I think we should investigate.' Evangeline led the way into the kitchen. A couple of the minions who were working with the tea-trays sent us nervous smiles as we approached the work centre.

Meta was up to her elbows in the cooking arrangements. Light glinted off the razor-sharp knife as she slashed at something limp on the chopping-board. She was normally so fastidious that I was startled to see that her hands were blackened and black spots disfigured her white apron.

'My, that looks . . . interesting.' Poker-faced, Evangeline

stared down at the chopping-board; only the slight narrowing of her eyes betrayed that she was less than pleased by what she saw.

'Yes, doesn't it?' I tried to convince myself that Meta couldn't possibly be chopping up fingers, or boneless unmentionable parts of the anatomy. 'Uh . . . what is it?'

'I'm sorry.' Meta turned harassed eyes on us. 'It's Mr Farraday's orders. He says the meals have got to be more atmospheric from now on. He wants to create a mood of claustrophobic intensity as the filming approaches a climax.'

'She doesn't want to know *why*.' Evangeline spoke slowly and clearly, as though interpreting my words for a foreigner. 'She wants to know *what*—and so do I.'

'It's cuttlefish, baby cuttlefish.' Meta picked up what I could now identify as bits of tentacles and tossed them into a pot. 'Cooked in its own ink and then it's going to be served up as part of a risotto or pilaff. And I might as well tell you—' She looked at her hands despairingly. 'It's going to turn out black. I don't know what the crew will say, but Job insisted. He gave me the recipe himself.'

'It looks as though all that's missing is eye of newt.' Evangeline regarded the chopping-board thoughtfully. 'Tonight, eh? Suppose someone is allergic to cuttlefish ink?'

'The only other choice on the menu—' Meta's voice rose in incipient hysteria—'is Capon's Blood Omelette. I drew the line at using chicken blood—and I wish I could be sure that ink isn't a cuttlefish's version of blood—but half red wine and half tomato sauce will make it look good and bloody.'

'It certainly will,' I murmured. It all sounded revolting. Job would be lucky if Fabian was the only one to walk off the film.

'And we had a dozen cases of Bull's Blood wine delivered this morning,' Meta continued wildly. 'Job says that's all we're to drink from now on.'

'Job is going to have a lot to answer for,' Evangeline said.

'Him and his atmosphere! As though the weather wasn't atmosphere enough.' I looked towards the window. A solid

90

dark fog had wrapped itself around the building. 'I may never eat again.'

'*And* he wants evening meals served by candlelight.' Having started her tale of woe, Meta seemed unable to stop. 'And I don't know what the insurance company will say if anything should happen—'

'It might improve the situation if people can't actually see what they're eating,' Evangeline said. 'And if he keeps the Bull's Blood flowing freely enough, people might even forgive the name. Just the same . . .' We exchanged glances in silent agreement. We had been warned.

'We must have a word with Dear Griff,' Evangeline said. 'I'm sure he'll give us a lift down to the town. There are so many errands I must attend to—I've been putting them off for far too long.'

'Me, too.' I was right with her. 'Don't wait dinner for us, Meta. We'll snatch a bite in town.'

'I don't blame you,' Meta said sorrowfully. 'Just remember, this wasn't my idea.'

We escaped from Griff at the post office, pleading unspecified but urgent and complicated business to attend to. He wanted to take us to dinner, but I'm afraid we gave him the impression that we were going back to the hotel for dinner. Since he hadn't heard about the menu, he believed us.

After fond farewells, with Evangeline practically swearing a blood oath that next time she'd visit *Yesterday's Dreams*, we bustled into the post office and bought some stamps— you can always use extra stamps—until Griff had had time to drive away.

'It's warmer outside than inside,' Evangeline said as we strolled along Baxtergate towards the River Esk.

'That's because we're out of that howling wind. Only Job could have stranded us in that ark of a place, miles from civilization.'

'It's not that far, actually. It just seems like it because it's straight up. He thinks he's Cecil B. de Mille handing down tablets from a mountain top.'

91

'Yes.' Her metaphor was mixed, but I knew what she meant. The shops were closing but their windows were still brightly lit and I realized how much I had missed being in the centre of busy streets. People smiled at us as we passed, I wasn't sure whether it was because they recognized us, because they were amused by our costumes, or because they were naturally friendly, but it was very pleasant.

'Brrr! Here's your wind!' We had come out at the street winding along beside the river and the difference was noticeable. On the top of the great cliff on the other side of the Esk, the ruins of the Abbey stood out blackly against the dark sky. It would be a lot colder and windier up there.

Quite a few people were hurrying around a corner and we followed them into Flowergate. Almost immediately we were confronted by another hill, small but steep.

'No wonder this town produced so many seafarers,' Evangeline said. 'After all these hills, the sheer *flatness* of the ocean on a good day must have been irresistible.'

We moved away from the hill and back to the Marine Parade where we took the next turning along. This one stayed on the level.

'Haggersgate—' Evangeline squinted up at the sign. 'The way we've been blown about by the wind, I feel that we could pass for the Hags.'

'There's bound to be some place to eat if we keep going.' I tried to smooth my wild hair and looked around hopefully as we walked along. There were several places, but they seemed to be closed. This was probably a lively area in the height of summer; we were definitely Out-of-Season now.

'You can't get away from that river!' Evangeline said crossly as Haggersgate ended and we found ourselves back by the water.

'This is the harbour.' Small boats and fishing craft were moored along the harbour wall. Our road led on to one of the pair of long concrete arms cradling the harbour and ending in lighthouses. It must have been a pleasant walk— in summer.

'I'm not going out on that!' Evangeline halted.

'Neither am I—but that looks like a row of restaurants

just ahead. One of them must be open, there are lights.'

Grumbling, she allowed herself to be coaxed along. There were lights and bustle at the top of a long flight of steps. As we hesitated, some people came out laughing and I realized how long it had been since I had seen anyone so cheerful. It had to be a good sign.

'Let's go in here.'

'Up those stairs?' Her sigh was perfunctory. 'Remember we'll have to come down them again.'

'Well, if we stay sober, we ought to be able to manage it.'

'Very funny.' But Evangeline was mollified by the time we were seated at a table for two beside an open fire—which didn't blast smoke into the room—and sipping chilled white wine while we devoured perfectly cooked and utterly delicious fish and chips.

'This is better,' she admitted. 'Much better.'

'Anything would be better than the menu Job ordered for tonight. Him and his atmosphere!'

'I hope you've packed your earplugs. There should be a bumper crop of nightmares tonight.'

'Don't!' I shuddered. 'Those kids are overworked, over-tired and ripe for an outbreak of hysteria.'

'And I'm not feeling so well myself.' Evangeline was not to be outdone. 'I think it may be time to slip away for a restorative weekend in London.'

'We can't do that right now,' I protested. 'Job's going to wrap up the principal filming over the next few days.'

'You can do as you like, Trixie—' Evangeline raised a hand to her forehead. 'But if this headache gets any worse, I shall simply *have* to consult a Specialist in London.'

'You'll never get away with it!' Job knew all about that one, too. It was as old as Fabian's trick, although harder to disprove when medical certificates started flying through the air.

'Won't I?' It had been a mistake to challenge her. 'Just watch me!'

If both of them walked out, there went the picture. Even if they came back, the momentum Job had built up would be lost. We might not like it, but I knew that the tensions and cross-currents Job was creating among us all would show themselves on the screen—and to our advantage. Any let-up in tension could spoil it. We had to put up with his ideas, even though he was tightening the screw another turn with the 'atmospheric' menus. He'd be reading us all ghost stories by firelight next! He didn't care what he did to our nerves so long as he got his own way—and now both Fabian and Evangeline were threatening his authority. That could be dangerous. Except that he didn't know about Evangeline—yet.

'Oh, well—' I tried for a careless tone. 'If you're not around when Job wants to shoot your scenes, he'll probably give them to Griselda.' Or he might give them to me, but I knew better than to make that suggestion.

'Grisly has enough scenes!'

'And maybe Job has.' That was another possibility. Anyone who has come to the cinema from the stage must always harbour the suspicion that films are shot out-of-sequence, higgeldy-piggeldy and practically upside-down just to disorient the actors and keep them off-balance. When your first day on the set can find you in a torrid love scene with a man you've just been introduced to, and the final day's shooting can consist of endless shots of your hands dipping a cup into the dishwater, you neever know where you are—and if you think you do, you're probably wrong.

Job had been working with all of us separately and together. It was possible to guess just how many key scenes he had finished—particularly when you considered what could, and often did, happen at the editing stage. The film that went into the cutting-room wasn't always the same film that came out. None of us had seen any of the rushes. If Job had shot enough material, the picture could withstand any number of disappearing actors.

And Job had stolen a few scenes when we were not aware that we had been on camera, like the night of Griselda's arrival, when we had dragged Alanna in out of the storm. He had never suggested a retake of that, so he must have considered it satisfactory. How many other scenes had he filmed by trickery and stealth?

I remembered that Koji had been in the vanguard of the early experiments with infra-red lighting techniques. You don't hear anything about infra-red now that everything is shot in colour. But Job was shooting this in black-and-white.

Furthermore, there had been several successful films whose stars had died before the end of shooting. An awful lot could be done with a back view and a dubbed-in voice.

Fabian had better watch his step; he wasn't indispensable. And maybe Evangeline wasn't, either. Job was a lot more cold-blooded than he tried to appear—especially where his films were concerned.

'I don't know—' Evangeline had the abstracted inward-gazing look of someone who had just heard of a birth-announcement within the first year of marriage and was counting off the months. 'Maybe Job *does* have most of the key scenes in the can. But he hasn't done any of the stunts yet.' Her lips twitched. 'I'm looking forward to Fabian's reaction when he has to do the famous scene of crawling head first down the wall of the castle.'

'That's easy—and you know it. They'll paint a brick-front canvas, put it on the floor, he'll crawl over it with a wind machine blowing his cloak out and they'll turn the film the other way round so that he seems to be vertical instead of horizontal.'

'True.' Her lips still twitched. 'But what would you like to bet that Job lets Fabian sweat a bit before he explains the trick? I don't have the feeling that he likes Fabian very much. No doubt he has his reasons.'

I didn't answer. I was remembering that sketch of a figure in one of our costumes somersaulting through the air above the Church Stairs. I had managed to push the frightening image to the back of my mind during the past frantic week. Neither Evangeline nor I would go anywhere near that stunt, but someone else . . . someone unwary . . .

Suddenly, I was very much afraid that the worst was yet to come.

95

The waitress appeared just then and effortlessly talked us into a rich chocolate dessert—very rich and very comforting. After the coffee, we decided that the walk to the taxi-rank would do us good and work off a few calories. We'd have been willing to walk all the way home if it hadn't been for those hundred-and-ninety-nine steps.

The wind had abated; consequently, the fog had thickened, shrouding the streetlamps and muffling sounds. We walked along Pier Road and then Marine Parade on the harbour side. The tide must have been coming in, for we could hear the splash of waves against the sea wall. There were no other people around now though, the streets were completely deserted. Everyone was safely home, having their meals and watching television—

'What was that?' Something made me jump.

'What?' Evangeline paused and listened. 'I don't hear anything.'

'Sorry, this place is getting on my nerves, I guess.' I looked up at the sky, but all I could see was fog. Even the ever-brooding presence of the Abbey ruins had been blotted out. I would have been willing to bet that, above the fog, the moon was full. It was that kind of night.

'There it is again! Didn't you hear that?'

'Hear what?' Evangeline stopped and turned on me in exasperation. 'Just what do you think you keep on hearing?'

'I don't know. It sounds—' I didn't like to say it. I knew what her reaction would be.

'Trixie—'

'It sounds like something growling. Like a gigantic animal . . . growling . . .'

'An enormous hound, by any chance?' Her face was a blur in the fog, but her voice was sarcastic. 'You're forgetting your lines, Trixie. That's supposed to be "the *footprints* of an enormous hound", not the growl—*oh!*'

'You see?' It had come again and she'd heard it this time all right. 'Maybe—' Something Barney had said came back to me. 'Maybe it's the Padfoot!'

And only those who were about to die could hear its ghostly roar. We had both heard it now.

'Nonsense!' Evangeline said robustly. 'It's far more likely to be one of those ghastly pit bull terriers being taken to a dogfight.'

'That happens down in London. We haven't seen any fighting dogs up here.' In fact, I'd noticed with pleasure how nice it was to see people with sloppy old mongrel pet dogs again—and all of them had been on leads. The thing growling in the fog behind us didn't sound as though it was on any leash.

The growl sounded again. Louder. And closer.

'Keep moving,' Evangeline said abruptly. 'Hurry up! And don't clatter your heels like that!'

'Animals don't go by sound—they go by smell. And we're both reeking with French perfume!' The thing was closer.

'Save your breath!' Evangeline grabbed me by the wrist and we began running.

'This way!' I guided us across the street and into the partial shelter of the buildings on the other side.

The growl was much more of a roar this time—and a lot closer. I glanced over my shoulder and saw two enormous slitted yellow eyes.

'*Faster!*' I was pulling Evangeline along now. We sped past the dark turning into Haggersgate—no good, that would simply take us back parallel to the way we had come and dump us back on the Pier Road. We'd be behind the thing—and it might turn and run us into the sea.

Evangeline looked over her shoulder and yelped. She'd seen the eyes now, too. We were neck-and-neck racing past Flowergate—too steep, even when we hadn't been in this winded condition.

'Down Baxtergate!' I choked. The ancient pedestrian precinct was lined with shops—surely there must still be something open, someone who could come to our aid.

As we dived into Baxtergate, there was a roar like a beast about to pounce. I thought we'd been running before, but there was one last effort left in us. The ground seemed to have turned into a trampoline beneath our feet as we hurtled along. At the same time . . .

'That was a motor,' I gasped. 'I'm sure . . . that was a motor.'

'Whatever it is . . . we're goners if . . . it gets us!'

She was right. Whatever it was, we were its target for tonight. But not if we could help it.

'Ahead!' An oasis of light glowed through the gloom. A shop—still open.

In a final burst of speed, we reached it and hurled ourselves against the door. It sprang open and we tumbled into the shop.

Outside, a long dark shape roared over the spot where we had been running just a split-second ago.

We clung to each other, gasping for breath and trembling. That had been close. Too close.

'Ladies, are you all right?' The shopkeeper hurried forward, his face white with alarm. 'You didn't get the licence number, I suppose? Silly buggers turn this place into a racecourse after dark. Let me get you a chair—' He bustled into a back room and returned with a chair in each hand.

'Thank you.' I was getting my breath back, although my heart was still thudding wildly. Evangeline sank down into her chair with a nod of thanks and closed her eyes.

'Water—' the man said and hurried away again.

'Brandy—!' Evangeline croaked a correction, but he was already gone.

'Why?' I whispered in the moment we had to ourselves. She shook her head. She didn't know either.

'Here we are, ladies.' The water was cold and delicious, I drained my glass without coming up for breath. Evangeline sipped at hers like a lady, only the faint frown betraying her discontent that it was not brandy.

'Better?' The man was hovering anxiously. 'Can I get you anything else?'

'Please—' I looked at the darkness outside the window and my courage failed me. I wasn't going out on foot again tonight. 'Could we call for a taxi from here?'

'Of course, of course. I'll ring them—and if I can't raise anyone, I'll drive you home myself.'

'How kind of you.' Evangeline was beginning to revive;

she looked around with interest. 'And how lucky we were that you're still open. It's an ill wind . . .' We had found refuge in a liquor store.

'I was just getting ready to close. I'll see about that taxi. Not that I mean to hurry you, ladies.'

'Not at all. We're quite anxious to get back.' Evangeline strolled towards the shelves, humming under her breath.

'An excellent opportunity to replenish our supplies, I think.' She selected two bottles of cognac.

It wasn't a bad idea. I took one for myself, plus a bottle of Scotch. In fact, since we were getting a lift back, I added one of those useful three-litre boxes of white wine. We'd be sick of the sight of Bull's Blood before Job was through.

'Oh, ladies—' The shopkeeper was startled at his unexpected last-minute sales. 'You don't need to do that.'

'Oh yes we do,' Evangeline said grimly. 'Believe me, we do.'

CHAPTER 11

We slept late the next morning, having warned Job that we would. He had not been exactly sympathetic when we saw him last night. He had been coming up from the canteen as we swept through the front door with our booty.

'Job—we've just been attacked!' Evangeline greeted him.

'Congratulations! I always knew you two weren't past it.'

'Not that kind of attack, you fool!' I thought Evangeline was going to hit him.

'Someone tried to run us down in a car,' I explained quickly. 'In the town. Just now.'

'No kidding?' Job looked momentarily concerned. 'But you're OK? Sure, you are. I can see that.' He gave us a wide, apparently toothless smile.

'Job! Your teeth are all black.'

'It's the ink,' he said. 'The stuff is as bad as blueberry pie for staining teeth. But you gals missed a great meal.'

'Oh no we didn't.' Evangeline turned to the taxi-driver, who was carrying the large cardboard carton with our purchases. 'If you'd just take that upstairs, please. Trixie, show him the way.'

'Just one flight.' I led the way up to our suite, the driver trailing me cheerfully. After what Evangeline had tipped him, he'd have carried our shopping all the way up to the attic without a murmur.

Below us, I could hear Evangeline laying down the law to Job. It had been a long time since he'd been on the receiving end of one of her temperaments and he was demoralized in no time. As I opened the door to our suite, I could hear Job agreeing that we could sleep as late as we liked in the morning.

'You can set it down over there.' I indicated a corner. 'Thank you.'

'Thank *you*,' he said happily and left.

Without an audience, I could let go. My knees gave way abruptly and I dropped into an armchair. I had begun trembling again. A low growl seemed to reverberate in my ears. I had the impulse to run again—but I was already home and safe.

Safe? It had turned out to be a car that was chasing us, but we hadn't imagined the rest of it. There had been growls and there had been yellow slitted eyes. And I had been carefully primed with stories of the Padfoot, the ghostly monster prowling the dark streets at night.

Someone had rigged up that car to make the Padfoot spring to mind. Maybe they thought they could frighten us into heart attacks that way—literally scare us to death. Or maybe they wanted us to come back to the Castle babbling of supernatural beings stalking us, so that the others would begin to doubt our stability, perhaps even our sanity.

Who would have believed us if we had come back babbling a story like that? Who would want to do such a thing to us? And why?

The how was easy: Special Effects.

*

100

By the time we had our second cup of coffee in the morning, the world was looking a little better. Griselda was already downstairs filming the shots we weren't needed in, so we had a bit of privacy. We had discussed the events of last night exhaustively and agreed that we would not mention the Padfoot, nor give any indication that the thought of such a thing had for one moment crossed our minds.

A car trying to run us down was bad enough. There had been flickers of disbelief in some eyes at the story as it was.

Furthermore, it might throw whoever-it-was off his stride if he thought we had not even noticed his elaborate adjustments to his vehicle. It might stop him trying such tricks in the future if he thought they were unappreciated.

On the other hand, it was possible that some local maniac had been behind the wheel. Some bored teenager, perhaps, who thought it was funny to turn his jalopy into a Batmobile or Padfoot and go out to frighten young girls. He might have taken a practice swing at us just because we were there.

'There's no point speculating—' Evangeline set down her coffee cup and rose to her feet. 'Either it will happen again, or it won't. Maybe to someone else, or maybe to us again. We'll just have to wait and see. Meanwhile, I suppose it's time we reported to the set.'

Griselda was in a filthy mood. It showed in the vicious way she lashed out at poor Igor. There was too much enthusiasm in the kick that sent him hurtling backwards, somersaulting to the far side of the set.

Koji tracked the shot, chortling. It was obviously making good cinema. Igor was looking a trifle wan, though. I wondered how many takes they'd been through already.

'Cut!' Job spotted us.

'So, you deign to appear at last!' Griselda sneered. 'Such selfishness! You have no thought for poor Igor, who must work himself to a frizzle because you are not here for your scenes.'

'I think that's frazzle—' Job broke off as Griselda sent him a look that would have felled an ox.

Igor picked himself up slowly and dusted himself off, an

odd little smile on his lips. 'I am glad that you have arrived,' he told us. 'I was growing weary. I am no longer in the sprightly middle-age when *I* went tumbling through Transylvania with the circus.'

'Oh, but you were magnificent!' Griff was blissful. He had been provided with a canvas Director's chair (or had he brought one from his own collection?) and was seated near the principal camera. 'Magnificent! I don't know whether I liked Take 3 or Take 7 better.'

'We can use them all,' Job said. 'They're all great. We'll intercut with stuff we've already filmed. It will make a good running gag.'

'Yes . . .' Griff nodded judiciously. 'Yes, that will work very well.' There was no mistaking it, he was in seventh heaven all right.

I was pleased for him. For about thirty seconds. Then an unnerving idea slid into my mind.

I had toyed with the idea of a local nutter being last night's culprit—and here he was. As local as they come. And as much of a nutter?

Certainly, he must know enough about special effects as anyone in the business. And the Padfoot had been a basically simple camouflage—just a bit of paper and masking tape over the headlights—easily applied and easily removed. Nor would it have been too difficult to rig up something that would broadcast a growl.

Griff had known we were in the town, he had taken us there himself. It would not have required any great deduction on his part to suspect that we were probably going to have dinner somewhere in town. There were only a limited number of restaurants still open out-of-season; all he'd need to do was cruise around looking for us. A simple process of elimination like looking through windows—most restaurants were on ground-floor level—and he'd know where we weren't, which would give him a pretty good idea of where we *were*.

And . . . and . . . the probabilities were mounting up. And I'd liked the little man. I thought he liked all of us, too. What could he possibly have against us?

Or was it completely impersonal? A matter of business? Would our artefacts, like artists' paintings, become more valuable once we were dead?

'I trust I am no longer needed—' Igor looked to Job—'and I may retire to a hot bath and see to my bruises?'

'Sure, sure!' Job waved a hand dismissively. 'You go along. I'll be working with the girls for the rest of the day.'

'Splendid! Splendid!' Griff seemed genuinely delighted. Would he really have tried to kill us last night when he was looking forward to watching us work today? Or might he be one of those peculiar schizoids whose left hand didn't know what its right hand was doing?

'All right—places, girls!' Job interrupted my brooding. 'Where's make-up? I want some shadows on Trixie's cheeks—try to make her look like she's got cheekbones. Gimme some hollows there.'

The make-up artists moved forward and surrounded me, another team converged on Evangeline. I saw Igor slide away towards the stairs; he was off-guard and not bothering to conceal his limp now that he thought no one was watching. Half way up the stairs, he hesitated and looked up.

Lora was descending slowly, again clinging to the banister and carrying something that looked too heavy for her. She was paler than ever, almost grey.

Suddenly, I wondered whether she could be pregnant. That would explain her blithe assurance that Job was going to marry her. If so, she was having a hard pregnancy, but perhaps she thought it was worth it.

Actually, Job ought to marry her out of sheer flattery. It must be a long time since any woman had thought he was worth that much effort.

Igor continued up the stairs and out of sight, while Lora paused at the bottom of the stairs to catch her breath.

'Here, let me help you.' I couldn't stand by and see her struggle. I shook off the minions and went over to her. 'I can take that.'

'No!' She pulled the box out of my grasp. 'It's all right.' She was too quick, too defensive. 'It's not heavy.'

It wasn't. I'd been able to tell that in the brief moment

it was in my grasp. Nor was it an awkward shape. There was no need to make such heavy weather of carrying it. Either Lora was even weaker than she looked, or she was trying to make Job feel guilty.

I could have told her that was wasted effort. Job wouldn't recognize guilt if it walked up and bit him on the ankle.

'It's for Griff.' Lora offered an explanation as an apology. 'Just a few things Job got together to donate to his Exhibition. There'll be more later. Job thinks it's a great idea. They're working out some kind of exchange deal together.'

I instantly began to worry about Griff, he was far too much of an innocent to get involved in any deal with Job.

'Trixie!' Job bellowed, as though he could sense my silent criticism. 'Get back on your mark! We're ready to shoot.'

'Coming!' I picked up my skirts and dashed for the chalk mark opposite Evangeline. As we swung into our first scene, I saw that Griselda had gone to sit beside Griff, who was plainly delighted by the attention. Lora brought the box over and gave it to him, which delighted him even more. I was looking at a very happy man. I wondered why it made the hair prickle at the nape of my neck . . . ?

Even with a late start, it seemed an inordinate length of time before we broke for lunch. Our enthusiasm for food diminished, however, when we reached the buffet.

Glasses of tomato juice and blood orange juice reposed in the trough of crushed ice. For the favoured few, of course, there were Bloody Marys at the bar. Job gestured to us with one, inviting us to join him, but the only part of that drink I could face was the sprig of celery in it. Evangeline gave him a haughty glare that implied she never touched the stuff, especially at midday, and we continued to case the buffet.

Halves of hard-boiled eggs were filled with red lumpfish caviar looking like coagulated—

'I don't think I'm hungry,' I said.

'Job goes too far,' Evangeline agreed. 'Method Acting is bad enough, but to order Method Cooking—!' She shuddered.

'Yeah.' There was too much tomato in everything,

making the shrimp in the Shrimp Creole look look like small twisted pieces of flesh weltering in blood. The black-skinned pieces of aubergine in the Ratatouille looked unspeakable. Even the Lasagne was made with tomato-tinted pasta. 'Do you think we could send out for sandwiches?'

'Let's try a raid on the kitchen first. There *must* be some food still unstained—' She caught herself. 'I mean, *uncoloured*, down there.'

'If we can get to it before they begin messing it around.' I followed her down the stairs and into the kitchen.

'Ah, Julian, dear boy—there you are!' He was sitting at the big trestle-table with Barney and Hobie. They had a large pot of coffee and an enormous plateful of ham-and-cheese sandwiches—that was more like it. 'I'm glad to see Job hasn't locked you in your room again.'

'No, he's not getting away with that again.' Julian leaped to his feet as we approached. I didn't like the way the others began gathering up the pieces of paper scattered around them. It was all right to tidy the papers into a neat pile—but why turn it face down?

'Er, would you care to join us?' Evangeline had already seated herself at the table.

'Dear boy, how kind!' She helped herself to a sandwich.

'We could use some coffee, too,' I suggested, sliding on to the bench myself.

'I'll get you a cup.' Julian surrendered gracefully. 'And you,' he added quickly as Evangeline opened her mouth.

He was looking a bit pale and wan, too. Or was it just that the food was so bright lately that everything and every-one else paled by comparison?

Julian set down our cups and saucers and poured coffee for us. The sandwiches were as delicious as they looked and I munched away contentedly. Somewhere in the back-ground I heard Meta giving complicated instructions about several things at once and marvelled at the way Job seemed able to surround himself with groupies who were willing slaves. I wondered if he bothered to pay them—and how much. Nothing like Union Scale, I'd bet. Maybe he hypno-tized them.

'Where are the others today?' Evangeline asked.

'Oh, around,' Julian said casually. 'A few of them have gone down into the town, but Fabian will be back in time for his scene with you. Alanna and her mother were planning to have dinner in town, as they won't be needed until morning.'

'Madame Defarge won't be needed at all,' Evangeline said crisply. 'I trust Fabian will soon find a way to let her know that.'

'I think she's getting the idea.' I remembered the dangerous flash of her eyes as Fabian had snubbed her. 'But she won't give way without a fight.'

'My money is on Fabian.' Evangeline took another sandwich and drained her coffee. 'I've seldom seen a more overbearing ego. I could feel sorry for Alanna—if she weren't such a cipher.'

Barney's jaw tightened, but he didn't say anything. I buried my nose in my coffee-cup, determined to stay out of this. Julian and Hobie didn't notice any undercurrents; they were too absorbed in their own concerns.

'More coffee, Trixie?' It was most unlike Evangeline to be so thoughtful. She tilted the coffee-pot over my cup—and missed.

'Ooops!' She snatched for something to mop up the splash of coffee on the table. Her hand alighted on a sheet of paper on top of the pile they had been trying to hide from us. There was no absorbency in it, but I knew by then that that hadn't been her main idea.

She dropped the page over the splash and looked down at it. Not by coincidence had it fallen sketch side up—and the familiar flying figures were tumbling through the air over the Church Stairs. Now it was out in the open.

'How interesting,' Evangeline said coldly. 'That reminds me—I haven't met any of the stunt people attached to this Unit. Or haven't they arrived yet?'

There was a long nasty silence.

'It's not that complicated a stunt,' Hobie said finally. 'Anyone could do it.'

'*Anyone?*' Evangeline raised an eyebrow. 'I, for one, could

106

not and *would* not do it. And neither would Trixie.' So now they knew, just in case they'd had any doubts about it.

'Of course not,' Julian said quickly. 'No one would expect you to. I believe Job is planning to have Lora double for you on this.'

'Lora?' I was shocked. 'Has she had any training for stunt work? Besides, she isn't well.'

'What's wrong with her?' Hobie was aggrieved at the prospect of losing his cherished special effect. 'She looks all right to me.'

'Then you can't have taken a good look at her lately. The poor kid is practically dead on her feet.' And that was too close to the truth to be comfortable.

'Job's a disgrace!' Evangeline snorted. 'At his age, he ought—'

Julian cleared his throat loudly. In the ensuing silence we heard the approaching footsteps. Julian cleared his throat again, just in case we'd missed the first signal.

'You OK?' Job asked solicitously. 'You're not coming down with a cold? I got some cough medicine in my room—'

'No, no,' Julian said quickly. He'd obviously been offered some of Job's home cures before. 'Just a slight tickle in my throat, that's all. It's gone now.'

'You sure? You don't want to take chances. An infection could spread through the unit like wildfire. We can't afford to lose any time right now. Maybe you ought to take something anyway.'

'He's not going to take anything unless he needs it.' Evangeline emphasized the 'he' ever so faintly. 'He's not a hypochondriac.'

'I suppose I am?' It didn't bother Job unduly, he'd been called worse things in his time. All true. 'Well, never mind that for now.' His smile would have done credit to an alligator. 'Are we ready to get back to work?'

'Of course, Job,' Evangeline said sweetly. 'We're always ready.' Her fingers drummed on the sketch. 'Within reason.'

'Oh, that.' Job looked from Barney to Hobie to Julian,

obviously wondering how much they had told us. 'I've been meaning to have a little talk with you girls.'

'No!' Evangeline said. 'No, no, no!'

'It was just a thought.' Job shrugged. 'Of course, if you're *chicken*—' He glanced at us slyly to see how we would react to this insult.

We gave him the stony silence and basilisk glare.

'Actually,' he said, 'it's pretty much arranged for Lora to double for you. I just thought you might prefer to do your own stunts.'

'We didn't do them forty years ago,' Evangeline said. 'Why should we start now?'

'OK, Ok, have it your way.' He knew that we would. 'Lora will be glad to do it.'

Would she? There was a crash somewhere behind us and I turned to see Meta picking up pieces of crockery from the floor.

'I'm sorry,' she said, 'it slipped.' So had her mask. For one blinding instant, sheer hatred flashed out of her eyes at Job. Job, the slave-driver, forcing hapless minions into dangerous work with a callous disregard for their safety and health. Meta didn't look too well herself. I wondered how much unpaid overtime Job had been getting out of her. And for how much longer. The whole atmosphere was beginning to reek of Palace Revolution.

'OK.' Job had missed the expression on her face and shrugged off the broken plate. 'Just watch it, that's all. We've got an inventory for all this stuff and we don't want any extra charges when we move out.'

CHAPTER 12

By the time we shot the final scene of the day, Griff was the only one among us who was still fresh and cheerful. If the Palace Revolution broke out, I knew who was going to lead it: Evangeline. And I'd be right behind her.

Just because Evangeline had splashed a little brandy into

108

our cups of tea, Job had stopped referring to it as Tea Break and begun calling it Happy Hour. He thought he was funny.

'If I can tear you girls away from Happy Hour,' he called, 'how about getting back on the set?'

Griselda tore herself from Griff's side with a self-righteous smirk—*she* had been tea-total.

'Really, it's disgusting the way that woman is carrying on with that little man,' Evangeline said. 'I hope Igor beats her. Why isn't he here to keep her in line?'

'I think she finished him for the day this morning.' I suspected that Igor wasn't as strong as he tried to appear. Those jokes about his old war wounds rang true. 'All that kicking around—'

'I don't know how she gets away with it,' Evangeline brooded. 'And he still adores her.'

Griff was doing fairly well in the adoration line himself. He kissed Griselda's hand as she left him. Evangeline snorted loudly.

We took our places and the minions surrounded us and made us fit to be photographed. They backed off as Job roared out the preliminaries to the Take.

This was the scene where Griselda began to feel that we were a bad influence on our dear vampire nephew, being too sentimental at heart and encouraging him in his unlikely affections.

The scene was basically Griselda's and Evangeline's. All I was required to do was to wring my hands in the background. In truth, I was standing by to intervene if they looked like coming to blows—and I mean in real life. It was looking more likely by the moment.

It was close, but it didn't actually happen. Griselda delivered her final line and stalked off-screen. It had been one of her best tirades and she had every reason to feel that the scene belonged to her and was beyond stealing.

She had reckoned without Evangeline.

Moodily, Evangeline turned towards the mantelpiece and reached out for one of the carved jet figures at the end. I saw that it was the likeness of Griselda which had originally stood on one of the small tables. Someone must have moved it. Guess who?

I became aware that Koji was unobtrusively angling for a close-up of Evangeline as she stared down at the figure and lifted it to her mouth.

Then, with a sudden vicious movement, she thrust it into her mouth and snapped its head off. A long slow drop of blood appeared at the corner of her mouth and glided down her chin.

'CUT!' Job roared. 'CUT!'

'That vass not the vay ve rehearsed it!' Griselda shrieked.

'Great shot!' Koji enthused. 'Just great! Wait till you see it in the rushes, Job.'

'Perfect!' Griff gloated. 'That was perfect!'

Suddenly I realized that the figure had not been carved jet, but wax—and I knew where Evangeline had acquired it.

So did Griselda. She gave Griff a hostile look and detoured abruptly. She had been heading back to join him, now she made it plain that she wouldn't go near him with a ten-foot pole.

'You'll get an Academy Award for this one yet, Job,' Koji said. 'Just wait till they get a load of that!'

'Yeah, well.' Job considered. 'Maybe it wasn't the way we rehearsed it, but never mind, we'll let it ride.'

Griselda spat something furious and probably obscene in her rarely-used native tongue and marched from the room.

'I trust—' Evangeline spat the wax head from her mouth and tossed it contemptuously into the fireplace—'that will be all that is required of us today?'

'Yeah, sure,' Job said bemusedly. 'That wraps it for tonight.'

'Thank heavens,' I murmured. It had been a long day.

'Trixie and I—' Evangeline felt it, too—'will have a light repast in our suite. An omelette and toast, I think. A *plain* omelette,' she emphasized. 'No tomato paste—and *no garlic!*'

I didn't like the way a couple of the minions looked at us and then at each other when Evangeline vetoed the garlic, but I comforted myself by thinking that it couldn't go on for much longer. Another three or four days at this speed should see the location shooting finished and us out of here. Meanwhile, I agreed with Evangeline; I wanted a quiet evening in our own sitting-room—and no garlic in the food.

At least we were spared the garlic. But the peace and quiet didn't last very long. We were just ending our meal—admittedly, it had arrived rather late—when the shrieks and screams began overhead.

'This is *too* much!' Evangeline was at her most martyred. 'The omelette was cold, the white wine was warm—and now this!'

'It's the minions—' I was already opening the door. 'And it sounds like hysterics. I wonder what *they* had for dinner tonight?'

'Something revolting, I expect.' Evangeline closed the door behind us and we headed for the back stairs. 'Job never could order a decent meal.'

The top floor corridor was chaos. A whole flock of bats was swooping up and down, pursued by some of the men trying to capture them in pillow cases while a few of the girls, clutching at their hair, cheered them on. The more genuinely frightened lurked behind doors opened the merest crack so that they could monitor the situation and the whereabouts of the bats. The noise level was rising continuously.

'OK, OK, what the hell's going on here?' Job charged up the stairs, Lora in his wake.

'What is it?' Meta was on the landing below. 'What's the matter?' She sounded as though she might already have some idea.

'Everybody calm down!' Job's sudden appearance had a deflating effect on everyone except the bats, who continued to swoop and flutter. He watched them grimly for a moment, then turned to Meta, who had just reached the top of the stairs, panting slightly.

'I told you to get rid of those things!' he snapped. 'What happened to those exterminators you called?'

'They . . . they never came.'

'Why the hell not?'

'Haunted house . . .' It was barely a whisper, impossible to tell who had spoken.

'Cut that out!' Job whirled, glaring impartially at everyone in sight. One of the bedroom doors closed soundlessly.

'There's nothing wrong with this house—except the bats,' Job said. 'And we're getting rid of those as fast as we can.' He turned back to Meta. 'Get those exterminators here first thing in the morning!'

'They won't come,' she said faintly.

'They can't be that busy. Offer them double!'

'Why bother?' I was surprised at her stubborn resistance. 'You're not going to be here much longer. The bats don't get into the house often. Someone must have opened the trapdoor to the loft and stirred them up. See, they're going back to their roosts already.'

Sure enough, the hall was emptying of the creatures. As I watched, another one soared upwards and through a small opening in the ceiling. Others were disappearing through a window someone had opened at the end of the hallway.

'Who'd do a thing like that?' Blank faces stared back at him. Job shrugged, abandoning his query. 'Just get those exterminators here.'

'Don't you understand?' Meta was beginning to look desperate. 'I can't! They won't come!'

'Why not?'

'They're protected!'

'So, they're in no danger here.'

'Not the exterminators—the bats. You can't get rid of them. They're a protected species!'

'Wait a minute—' Job couldn't believe it. 'Are you telling me I can't get rid of the bats because *they're* a protected species?'

'Exactly.'

'Look, I can understand, maybe, if people get bats in their belfry, but what do they do when they get bats in their own house?'

'They put up with it.' Meta gave a wild despairing laugh. 'If a colony of bats takes up residence in your attic, all you can do is learn to get along with them. The law protects them.'

'You mean the bats have got more rights than you have?' Job shook his head. 'Jeez, what a country!'

There were only a couple of bats still flying around. One had attached itself to the edge of the trapdoor opening and was hanging upside down. Job eyed it gloomily.

'Jeez!' he said again.

'They don't do any harm, really,' Meta said apologetically. 'You'd get used to them . . . in time.'

'And we can't do anything about them?'

'Not a thing. You could be prosecuted if you hurt them or upset them.'

'Nobody cares if I get hurt or upset,' Job brooded. 'In fact, I'm pretty upset right now.'

'I'm sorry,' Meta said. 'But there's nothing anyone can do about it. It's the Law.'

'Great!' Defeated, Job started down the stairs, then paused to reassert his authority where he could. 'Hey, you guys!' he shouted. 'Break it up! The party's over! Back to your rooms! Come on, Lora, we've still got those script changes to go over.'

'Lora will be along later.' Evangeline put her hand on Lora's arm, stopping her. 'We want to talk to her ourselves for a few minutes.'

We gave Job time to get out of the way, then took Lora down to our suite.

'What's the problem?' Lora sank down on the edge of a chair.

'You are,' Evangeline said. 'You're not looking too well. I just thought you could do with a drink—and a break from Job.'

'Thanks.' Lora closed her eyes wearily. Her hand rose to her throat. 'I can't stay long, though. He'll take it—I mean, he gets nervous when he has to be alone. He likes somebody there all the time.'

And he'd take it out of her if she thwarted him in any

113

way. Effortlessly, we completed the sentence she had started and thought better of.

'Brandy, I think,' Evangeline prescribed. 'There's white wine, too, but since we can't chill it properly, it doesn't taste so nice.' She poured the brandy and brought it to Lora.

'I suppose we could ask Meta if we can store the white wine in the kitchen fridge,' I said. 'But it's a long way to go and get it when we want some.'

'And things stored in communal fridges have a way of disappearing.' Evangeline had also had long experience with the light-hearted, if not light-fingered, habits of film units.

'I can help you there.' A few sips of brandy had brought some colour back to Lora's face and she was reviving. 'Job has his own refrigerator in the suite. He's kind of possessive about it and won't let me store my Cokes in it, but he can't object if *you* want to put some wine in it. And we're on the same floor, so it would be easy for you to get some whenever you want.'

'How very kind of you, my dear.' Evangeline spoke so smugly, I suspected that this was what she had had in mind all along in inviting Lora back for a drink . . . and a few hints.

'No problem.' But the shadows behind Lora's eyes made me doubt that. Job was not a good man to cross, even in minor matters. I hoped she wasn't putting herself in any . . . difficulty by doing us this favour. Job might not like our popping in and out of his suite to use his fridge. On the other hand, it was quite true that Job was anxious to keep us happy, so he might not mind our taking an advantage he wouldn't allow others. Well, not very much.

Lora didn't stay long and went off with the wine box, saying it would fit neatly into a corner of the fridge and Job probably wouldn't even notice it was there. She sounded as though she hoped so. It would save making explanations.

'Just the same, I don't like it, Trixie,' Evangeline said, as the door closed behind Lora.

'She isn't well,' I agreed. 'I just hope she doesn't collapse before we've finished here. And we've *got* to speak to her about not letting Job talk her into trying any stunt work, although I could see this wasn't the moment to bring up the matter.'

'Not that.' Evangeline wriggled her shoulders expressively. 'Although you have a point-and-a-half there. Job wouldn't notice there was anything wrong with the girl until she dropped dead at his feet. No—' She cut off the remark I was about to make.

'No, I mean all those bats. There was a mass invasion of them. It wasn't natural that so many should find their way down through that trapdoor. Not unless someone was up there behind them—driving them down.'

'But why? And who?'

'Do you know, I wouldn't put it past that Fabian. Just to make life more difficult for everyone.'

We had every right to expect that what was left of the evening would be peaceful—and yet we felt curiously reluctant to shed our costumes and lounge around in our dressing-gowns as we usually did.

Perhaps because the wind was rising again. Little puffs of smoke eddied down the chimney and out into the sitting-room. At this point, I was ready to count my blessings: at least it was smoke and not some of our protected bats.

Evangeline settled to a game of solitaire and I curled up with the *Whitby Gazette*. Neither the cards nor the newspaper were enough to claim our full attention. There was an uneasy atmosphere in the room, as though we were waiting for something—but didn't know what.

It wasn't Griselda. She swept through the room with an abstracted look and scarcely glanced at us. The indifference was mutual. Neither of us asked her if she'd had a pleasant evening.

'I am fatigued.' She paused to arch herself in the doorway, presumably just to keep in practice. 'I go to sleep now.'

'Good.' Evangeline transferred three cards from one pile to another, then shamelessly peeked at the card under the card she turned over. It was her firm theory that you couldn't cheat if you were the only one playing.

'Good night.' I flapped the *Whitby Gazette* at Grisly and she turned and disappeared into her own room. I returned to the paper.

Honestly, I don't know why there aren't more murders in the world! The paper had columns of Birthday Greetings and it seemed to be the fad to illustrate each greeting with a childhood picture of the victim—with special glee attached to those who'd attained fifty years and upwards. I'd have killed anyone who did that to me. So would Evangeline, only she'd have thoroughly maimed them first.

I was about to draw her attention to this revolting local habit when we heard a pounding at the front door. Someone was shouting incoherently, the doorbell began to shrill again and again. Then the door slammed and feet thudded up the stairs. The shouts turned into our names. The frantic pounding was on our door.

'I knew it!' Evangeline surged to her feet, scattering cards all over the floor. 'This night isn't finished with us yet!'

I beat Evangeline to the door and opened it. Griff staggered into the room and barely stopped himself from falling.

'Oh, thank goodness, thank goodness!' He looked from one of us to the other. 'You're all right! But—' Terror distorted his face. 'Where's Griselda? Is *she* all right? Where is she?'

'In her room.' I couldn't imagine why she hadn't appeared. She had hardly had time to get to sleep—and no one could sleep through all this commotion.

No one else was sleeping through it. The hallway was filling with minions and Job pushed his way through them, followed by Julian and Barney. Mrs Bright and Alanna were hovering behind them, as though uncertain whether to join the crowd scene.

'What is it?' Job demanded. 'What's wrong now?'

'Everything!' Griff seemed on the verge of tears, he stared around wildly. 'I must see Griselda. I must satisfy myself that she's safe!'

'I don't see why she should sleep when the rest of us

116

can't!' Evangeline went over to Griselda's door and rapped on it.

'Why shouldn't she be safe?' Job seemed to take the remark personally, which reminded me . . .

'Where's Lora?' I asked.

'What am I—an information bureau? The kid's asleep, she had a rough day. She's dead to the world.'

'Griselda!' The words galvanized Griff afresh. He leaped across the room to join Evangeline in hammering at Griselda's door. 'Miss von Kirstenberg! Griselda!'

'Yes? Yes? What is it?' The door opened slowly and Griselda stepped forward to drape herself in the doorway, displaying to its best advantage an impossibly glamorous black cobweb lace nightgown and negligee set.

We might have known it! Evangeline and I exchanged glances. *That* was what she had been doing while poor Griff was worrying about her: changing into her glamourwear. I'd have bet anything that when she went to bed she wore a long-sleeved full-length flannelette nightgown like the rest of us. The way the draughts whistled down the chimneys and through cracks around window frames, she would have had to be suicidal not to. But she wasn't going to let Griff know that. It was bad enough that she had been caught with a sleep mask and less-than-glamorous ensemble the first night the bats had swooped.

'Oh, thank heavens!' It looked natural to Griff, poor innocent. In fact, he was dazzled—as he was meant to be. 'Thank heavens you're all right!'

'Of course I am all right.' Griselda gave him a lazy smile and arched her back sinuously—like a boa constrictor about to wrap itself around its prey. She looked around at the others and her smile faded slightly. 'But why are all these people here?'

'Good question,' Job said. 'OK—' He turned to the crowd. 'Clear out! There's nothing to see. Back to your own business—if any.' He began shooing them towards the door. 'Come on, get outta here!'

Julian and Barney sidestepped the mass exodus and came to stand beside me. Alanna tried to stay, but pinioned by her mother on one side and Fabian on the other, she was led away like a prisoner, throwing a despairing backward glance at Barney.

'That's better!' Job slammed the door behind everybody and turned back to Griff. 'Now, what's all the panic?'

'I've been burgled!' Griff's voice rose with astonishment and indignation. 'I can't believe it, but I've been burgled!'

'Burgled? You?' Job couldn't believe it either.

'I got back to *Yesterday's Dreams*, after spending the day here. At first I didn't realize there was anything amiss. There was no sign of a break-in. Perhaps I left the pantry window open . . .'

I heard Julian sigh, the deep disillusioned, resigned sigh of a police officer who has heard this so many times before and despairs of Joe Public ever learning any common sense.

'I made myself a cup of hot chocolate and carried it into the parlour to sit and read the evening paper—and that was when I discovered the burglary!'

'But—was anything taken?' I couldn't imagine what. One man's treasures were a houseproud man's throwaways.

'Yes—oh, yes!' His eyes filled with tears. 'When I saw it, I—I was so shocked I spilled my hot chocolate!'

'Have a brandy.' Evangeline's hospitable instincts were aroused. She moved to the decanter.

'Have you reported this to the police?' Julian's dormant instincts stirred, too. I'll bet it was the first time he'd thought about the police since he got here.

'Not yet. Oh, thank you—' Griff accepted the brandy and sipped at it gingerly. 'I will, but I had to come here first.'

'Why?' Job frowned. 'You don't think any of *us* did it?'

'No, oh no!' Griff was appalled at the idea. 'No. I came here because I had to be sure the ladies were safe. It was all so—so horrible, you see.'

'What was?' Julian was getting back into the swing of his almost-forgotten career. 'What did they take? What did they do?'

'They—' Griff turned to us. 'They stole your costumes!

118

Yours, Griselda—and yours, Evangeline. I didn't have any of your costumes, Trixie, but—' He spoke as though awarding me a consolation prize—or maybe the booby prize. 'But they took your dancing shoes.'

'Costumes?' Job was incredulous. 'They stole costumes?'

'But it was the *way* they stole them!' Griff blushed and looked at the floor. 'The . . . the replicas were . . . were stripped naked and . . . and hurled to the ground. And . . . and . . .' Fearfully, he risked a timid upward glance at Evangeline.

'And . . . Evangeline's replica was face down. And . . . and they had driven a knife between her shoulder-blades!'

CHAPTER 13

'Then it is elementary . . .' Griselda had once played the mysterious foreign lady against Basil Rathbone's Sherlock. 'One simply looks for a discerning critic.'

'Vandalism.' Absently, Julian caught Evangeline's arm as she started for Griselda.

'Or kids larking about.' Barney took a softer view. 'You'll probably get everything back when they're tired of clowning around with it. You'll find it stuffed into a rubbish bin down on the Front.'

'You ought to report this right away,' Julian said. 'Would you like me to come with you?' I sensed that he might actually be looking forward to visiting a police station again. It would make a pleasant contrast to being locked up with a word-processor.

'Yes . . . No . . . I don't know.' Griff finished his brandy and looked at us mournfully. 'I don't want to go back there and have to look at what they've done. Or even talk about it any more. Can't it wait?'

'The police don't have a conspicuous success rate on burglaries anyway.' Barney weighed in on Griff's side. 'Not in London, that is. Maybe up here they keep better tabs on all the local tearaways and can take an educated guess at who might have done it, but a few more hours shouldn't make much difference.'

'I—I'd be most awfully grateful if we could delay it a bit. Until I get over the worst of the shock. As long as you're all safe. I was so frightened when I saw what they'd done to the replicas—'

'You can stay here tonight,' Job said. 'You don't want to go back there right now. We can fix you up with a bed, plenty of space. In the morning, Meta and Lora can go back with you and help you clean up.'

And wouldn't they be delighted if they could hear Job casually volunteering their services like that? As though they didn't have enough to do around here. But Job was of the old male chauvinist pig generation and there was no point in trying to reconstruct him at his age.

'First, he has to report the burglary to the police,' Julian pointed out firmly. 'They'll want to go over the place before anyone disturbs the evidence.'

'Sure, sure. Did I suggest anything else?' Job was aggrieved.

'Oh, if I *could* stay the night—' Griff wasn't going to let the opportunity slip away. 'I'd be so grateful. I can just curl up in a corner anywhere. I don't suppose I'll sleep much anyway.'

'Not around here you won't!' Evangeline muttered. But the night was through with us now and I think we all knew it. Morning might be another matter.

'You must rest and not worry,' Griselda told Griff. 'I vill giff you another costume—' She gave a little shimmy and the black cobweb lace danced enticingly. 'Perhaps this one, *hein?*'

'Oh, Griselda! *Would* you?'

Evangeline snorted.

'Come on and we'll find you that bed.' Job obviously realized that the only way to get rid of Griff was to take his arm and forcibly remove him from the room. 'These girls need their beauty sleep. You too.' He glared at Julian and Barney.

'Oh yes, yes. Good night—I'm so glad you're safe. All of

you. *Good night, Ladies* . . . In an excess of hysteria, possibly brought on by the realization that he was going to spend the night under the same roof as his gods and goddesses, Griff burst into the song.

'*"We're going to leave you now . . ."*' floated melodiously down the corridor as the door closed behind them all.

Griselda shivered suddenly and I noticed with malicious glee that she had goosebumps on all that exposed flesh. Serve her right!

'Und zo, good night!' She almost tripped in her haste to retreat into her bedroom and change back into the comforting flannelette.

'I hate to admit it,' I told Evangeline, 'but she's got the right idea. I'm calling it a day, too. See you in the morning.'

Even Job was late on the set next morning. The rest of us were more or less assembled and waiting for him, if milling around drinking extra cups of coffee and nibbling Danish pastries could be so described. Actually, we didn't much care whether he put in an appearance or not. We could all use a day off.

Barney didn't look as though he'd had much sleep. I wondered if he'd drawn Griff as a room-mate.

Igor, on the other hand, was cavorting about high-spiritedly, completely recovered from his kicking-around yesterday. Even Grisly watched him with indulgent amusement, obviously still in a good mood from her chance to give the cobweb lace an airing last night.

'OK, folks!' Job came bounding down the stairs, full of life and the joys of a Spring only he seemed to believe was just around the corner. 'Are we ready to go?'

'Ready, Job,' Koji answered with enthusiasm. This film seemed to be rejuvenating elderly men while doing no good at all for the young females associated with it.

Lora, especially, looked drained and exhausted this morning. She also looked as though she might be having second thoughts about the desirability of being an Old Man's Darling rather than a Young Man's Slave. You had to choose your Old Man carefully. She hadn't. Even in his

121

dotage, Job would never be the doting type. She had wound up as an Old Man's Slave—the worst of both worlds—and Job was working her twice as hard as the most optimistic young man would dare. Perhaps she was also having second thoughts about making it permanent with a marriage ceremony. If she lasted that long. A nervous breakdown was lurking around her corner—Job had cornered all the Spring available.

Perhaps Lora ought to take lessons from Griselda, who had two attendant slaves of her own: Igor and Griff. They had all withdrawn to a quiet alcove now, Griff holding the script while Griselda and Igor rehearsed their lines. Griff had lost all traces of his distress of last night and was delighted with his new role as prompter. I suspected Julian was going to have problems trying to tear him away to go down to the police station and report his burglary.

'Where's Fabian?' Job called out.

'Fabian? Fabian?' Several voices took up the cry.

Alanna was there and ready, in her low-cut, throat-revealing velvet and lace evening gown. This was to be the pivotal After-the-Party scene in Dracula's study, where his honest intentions struggle with his baser instincts as he stares at that gleaming white throat. Then he decides that one little nip won't do any harm and he dives for it as the camera zooms in for a juicy close-up.

'Maybe it's too soon after breakfast,' somebody said and there was a ripple of nervous amusement.

'It isn't like Fabian to be so thoughtless of his fellow *artistes*,' Mrs Bright said. 'Shall I go up to his room and get him?'

Someone tittered. The nervous amusement could turn into hysterical laughter in another minute.

'Don't bother!' Job called them back to order. 'We'll start without him, that's all. Alanna, the scene begins with a tracking shot of you anyway. You've said good night to Dracula already, but you've had such a wonderful evening, you think you'll come down and thank him again because he gave you the pretty dress and the protection of his house—'

122

Alanna moved into place at the far end of the hallway. Minions converged on her, each doing their last-minute things, then retreated as Job shouted.

Lights dimmed, except for a following spot, cameras whirred, the clapperboard snapped and Alanna advanced along the corridor, almost on tiptoe, towards the closed door of Dracula's study. She tapped on it lightly and waited.

'CUT! Fine. We'll do a couple of close-ups now. Barney, go up and drag that bum outa bed! He saw his call-sheet, he knows he oughta be here now. Let him go without breakfast. Get him down here!'

Mrs Bright, trying to hide her annoyance that she hadn't been the one to be sent up to Fabian's bedroom—and after she had volunteered, too—rushed up to Alanna and tugged at her hair, pulling careless tendrils loose to frame the alabaster brow.

A backlight was set up behind Alanna to give her that haloed glow only black-and-white can bestow. Make-up came forward to dust a bit more powder in strategic areas. Grimly, the hairdresser tried to repair the helpful ravages of Mrs Bright, so that Alanna's hairstyle would correspond to the one she had worn when she started down the corridor. Koji changed the filters of his lenses.

'He isn't there,' Barney reported back.

'Check the kitchen. He's probably sneaking breakfast because he got up late.'

'Right!' Barney gave Alanna an encouraging smile and went off again.

'What?' I asked. Evangeline had muttered something under her breath, but she just huffed at me and refused to repeat it. It was probably just as well.

By the time they were ready for the next take, Barney was back shaking his head. Job didn't try to conceal his annoyance as he snarled the orders for the take to begin.

Alanna went through the full repertoire of maidenly emotions: doubt, hesitancy, misty-eyed recollection of an enchanted evening, then quivering resolve as she tapped on the study door.

Then we had more doubt, anxiety and maidenly blushes as her knock went unanswered. She turned away, as though to leave, then stopped, head cocked to one side, listening. Had there been an answering voice from within? She set her quivering hand on the doorknob and turned it.

'Good, good!' Job called. 'Keep going. We can get you entering, at least. Look ahead, into the room, he's sitting at his desk. He gets up and comes forward as he sees it's you—'

Alanna opened the door timorously and moved forward in accordance with his instructions, acting with her back, now that it was to the camera. Leaning forward, her body tilted forward to peer into the gloom, her shoulders hunched apologetically . . .

Suddenly her back snapped bolt upright. She took one step backwards and stood frozen in the doorway.

Then she began screaming.

'What the hell—?' Job started forward.

Evangeline was ahead of him. While the others stood stunned by the sudden shocking divergence from the script, Evangeline gained the doorway a full half-length ahead of me. Job fetched up a poor third.

'That boy—' Conscious of the still-whirring cameras, Evangeline remained in character. She caught Alanna by the waist and swung her into my arms where the girl collapsed, sobbing.

'That boy always was a messy eater!'

There was blood everywhere. The study was awash with blood. Pools of it soaking into the carpet. Gouts of it splashing the walls and bookcases. There were even crimson splashes on the ceiling.

'Jesus H. Christ!' Job croaked behind us.

I continued patting Alanna's back absently until Mrs Bright darted up and jealously wrenched her away from me. I was delighted to let her go. Unhampered, I moved forward to get a better view.

'Who'd have thought the old man had so much blood in him?' Trust Evangeline to show off her Shakespeare at a time like this.

Except that it wasn't an old man, although the emptied wizened husk on the floor beside the desk looked old. It was—it had been—Fabian.

'It's bad luck to quote *Macbeth*,' Job said automatically.

'Just how much worse do you think your luck can get?' Catching up her skirts and stepping carefully from one dry spot to another, Evangeline got close enough to the body to reach out gingerly and take hold of a wrist, searching for a pulse.

'CUT!' I shouted, realizing that the cameras were still working.

I turned to see Koji recording a slow pan of the shocked faces around us. He wasn't going to stop filming. My word wasn't good enough for him—Job paid the salaries. Besides, he could syndicate this footage to the TV news companies for more than Job was paying him for the entire film.

'Get an ambulance!' Evangeline straightened up, holding her bloodstained fingers away from her costume fastidiously. I gasped. Was it possible that there was still life flickering in that inert form? 'And for God's sake get Julian. Quickly!'

'Jeez, yes!' Job agreed. 'We're gonna need one helluva rewrite!'

'That's not the reason, you fool!' Evangeline snapped. 'Julian is a policeman. Fabian didn't do this to himself!'

There were shrieks and moans from those close enough to see and hear what had been going on. The hysteria began to spread outwards from them. At the edge of the crowd, someone—probably Barney, who seemed to have acepted the additional position of gofer—broke away and dashed upstairs, calling, 'Julian—'

'Here.' I had edged close enough to offer Evangeline a paper handkerchief. She accepted it gratefully and scrubbed at her fingers.

'*Not all the—*'

'Don't say it!' Job roared.

His voice disturbed something in a corner of the ceiling. I had thought it a particularly large and dark gout of blood,

125

but it dropped and spread black wings, wheeling through the air blindly, seeking escape. One of the errant bats. Its radar clicked into operation and it swooped out through the open door, raising more shrieks and howls from the minions crowding closer to the doorway and nearly starting a stampede.

Through it all I could see the eye of the camera peering, prying—and recording.

'Job,' I pleaded. 'Job, stop the cameras! Please, stop the cameras!'

'What?' Job looked around and became conscious of what was happening on the other side of the study door.

'CUT!' he roared. 'CUT! GODDAMNIT! CUT!'

There was a long slow moment before Koji obeyed. The last thing his camera recorded was Lora as she crashed to the floor in a dead faint.

CHAPTER 14

'I never thought I'd say this—' Evangeline was dabbing at her immaculate fingertips with a lace handkerchief now— 'but I do wish our dear sweet Superintendent Hee-Hee was here.'

So did I. At least he was all broken in to our little ways. The Whitby Police, while perfectly correct and polite, did not appear to be treating us with the gravitas we had come to expect. It wasn't that I actually *minded* being considered too old—if not too honourable—to be a viable suspect, but I got the feeling that Evangeline considered it a deadly insult. Furthermore, they weren't even particularly interested in our theories on the situation.

Even worse, they were looking definitely askance at Julian. More than just the understandable wariness at finding themselves faced with a London policeman, and one so completely out of context. What was he doing up here, mixed up with a mad film unit perpetrating yet another Dracula rehash? Was that any way for an honest hard-working policeman to spend his time? The phrase 'bent copper' was never actually uttered, but the impression hung in the air that Julian might, be somewhat warped, if not strictly bent.

Julian sensed all the unspoken criticism and reacted badly to it. This hadn't helped. Nor had Griff's delay in reporting his burglary, and Julian's collusion (as they viewed it) in that delay.

Fabian was still alive—but only just. At least, that was the story they were giving out. So it wasn't a murder inquiry yet. At best, it would turn out to be a fatal accident inquiry.

The minions had not made a policeman's lot any happier by insisting that Fabian had been the victim of the vampire bat which had swooped out of the study and disappeared— possibly changing back into human form when out of everyone's sight.

'I wish Julian would get back.' Suddenly I missed him terribly.

'Yes, I suppose we're lucky that we at least have Julian. But I'm afraid he doesn't carry any authority up here.'

'In fact, he's just one of the suspects.' There had been no mistaking the look in those narrowed eyes as they regarded their renegade colleague.

'Julian?' Evangeline considered the idea for a moment. 'It will do him a world of good,' she decided firmly. 'Seeing what life is like on the other side of the fence will enrich him as a police officer.'

'Mmm . . .' I doubted that Julian was taking such a philosophical view of it, wherever he was.

Where was he? And where was everyone else? I'd never heard the building so quiet. Even the wind had stopped howling down the chimney, although we were still getting the occasional puff of cinders into the room.

I went to the door, opened it, and stood listening. The only sound was a faint sobbing from the room Alanna shared with her mother down the corridor. I couldn't tell which woman was crying.

'This place is as cheerful as a morgue.' Evangeline joined me at the door. 'Let's go down to the canteen and see if they're going to feed us tonight or whether the whole place has gone to pieces.'

'Right.' It was as good 'an idea as any and lunch had been a bit slapdash. Not that anyone had been very hungry. After the sight of all that blood, the cheese sandwiches had been the most popular choice. I'd had peanut butter myself.

'*Tchach!*' Evangeline twisted her mobile features into an expression of distaste as we walked past Alanna's room. 'What hypocrisy!'

'She must have been partly in love with Fabian once.' I could sympathize with poor Alanna. 'Just because she no longer wanted to marry him, it doesn't mean that she can't feel anything at all for him.' If nothing else, it had been a nasty shock.

'You don't imagine that's *Alanna* crying?' Evangeline looked at me incredulously. 'Oh no! That's Madame Defarge bewailing her lost dreams of Empire. With Fabian dead, there's no way she'll be able to keep control over Alanna for much longer. Barney will never let her get away with the way she's been acting.'

'It didn't seem to me that Fabian went a bundle on it, either. He was showing signs of getting tough and taking over the whip hand himself. But—' I finally registered what she had said.

'Dead? You think Fabian is dead? Really? After the way those ambulancemen were working on him as they took him away? You don't think he's going to make it?'

'No one can lose that much blood and survive, I'm afraid.' Evangeline had played Nurse Edith Cavell, as well as several Army and Navy Nurses in World War II epics. Ever since, she had felt fully qualified to pronounce on all medical matters. 'Whatever it was, it breached the carotid artery. That's why the blood went everywhere. Arteries spurt—'

'Please!' I said faintly. The recollection was all too vivid. 'What do you mean—?' Something else struck me. '*Whatever* it was? Surely he must have fallen and cut himself?'

'Oh, Trixie, Trixie.' Evangeline shook her head. 'You've got to get over this *Little Mary Sunshine* complex of yours. It was *not* an innocent accident. And all is *not* for the best. And this is *not* the best of all possible worlds.'

'OK. So what's your interpretation?'

'Nothing good, I'm afraid.' Evangeline lowered her voice and looked around, although we were the only people on the staircase. 'I only caught the merest glimpse of the wound, but—' She lowered her voice still further, it was a whisper now. Unfortunately, Evangeline has a very penetrating stage whisper.

'But from the size and shape of the wound, I would say that the artery had been pierced by a *fang!*'

That silenced me—and her, too. We proceeded in thoughtful silence to the lower level and down the kitchen corridor. There was a low murmur of voices coming from the canteen, nothing like the usual cheerful uproar.

But even that low murmur stopped when we appeared in the doorway. Faces were turned towards us, then turned away again quickly. No one was willing to meet our eyes.

'Trouble, I think,' Evangeline said softly. I nodded.

There was a vacant table for two in the far corner. It was the one usually occupied by Job and Lora; Job always liked to sit where he could see everything that was going on in the room. At this point, it seemed like a good idea. We went straight to it, not looking left nor right, avoiding other eyes as busily as they were avoiding ours.

The trestle-table nearest us began to clear as we sat down. Noticing that the meals were unfinished, I told myself that nobody had much appetite today. I wasn't completely convinced.

Meta appeared behind the counter and waved, signalling us to remain seated and she would come and take our orders. She was a nice girl. I wondered again just how she had come to get herself mixed up with this motley crew. Whatever ambition she had thought she would fulfil, it could not have been to be Head of the Commissariat. I hoped Job would reward her suitably in his next production. Job . . .

Evangeline was in the chair Job usually occupied, back to the wall. I was in Lora's chair. Lora . . .

'Evangeline,' I said casually, 'just what *does* a wound made by a fang look like?'

'Just what you'd think,' she said impatiently. 'Small, round, a certain amount of coagulation around the edges . . .'

Several more nearby tables emptied hastily. It was their own fault. We had kept our voices low, they must have been deliberately eavesdropping.

'Perhaps we should change the subject.' Evangeline eyed the departing backs thoughtfully.

'I'm not sure it would make much difference.' The minions were predisposed to distrust us and had been for some time. Again, I remembered that head of garlic outside our door. To stop us from prowling at night? Did someone really imagine that would seal us in our suite? In a less secular age, they'd have been waving crosses at us.

Come to think of it, hadn't I seen a couple of slender gold neck chains bearing crosses around a few necks lately? I decided I was leaving the minute anyone began waving her cross in my face. I wasn't going to wait around for the scene where the peasants advance on the castle carrying flaming torches, shouting 'Rhubarb, rhubarb!' and jabbing the air with pointed stakes.

A couple of minions appeared in the doorway, looked around and spotted us and disappeared again.

'They really know how to make you feel great,' I muttered.

'I'm sorry I took so long.' Meta materialized beside our table. 'There was a spot of bother in the kitchen. It's all sorted out now—well, almost.' She tossed a harassed glance over her shoulder.

'Mutiny?' Evangeline was sympathetic. 'I'm not surprised. It's hard to keep help when—'

'It's a very simple menu tonight,' Meta cut in. 'We're closing the kitchen early. So it's cod and chips, toad-in-the-hole or spinach flan.'

Very simple. Evangeline and I exchanged glances. Very bloodless. And very English. Reassuringly English. Meta wasn't even calling it quiche instead of flan.

'The spinach flan, I think,' Evangeline said. I nodded agreement.

'I don't suppose you want any of the Bull's—the red wine?'

We both shuddered.

'No, no, I'm sorry. I shouldn't have mentioned it. Look—' Meta regarded us earnestly. 'Why don't you two go back upstairs? I'll serve you in your suite. It won't be any trouble.'

'And you'll be able to close the kitchen that much earlier—' Evangeline gave her a smile that told her she wasn't kidding us. 'If we weren't around scaring off the customers.'

'I didn't mean that.' But she did and we all knew it. Meta's face went a deep ugly red.

'Don't worry, my dear.' Evangeline pushed back her chair. 'We wouldn't dream of upsetting your arrangements. You can tell everyone it's safe to come back now!' She turned on her heel and swept out of the canteen. I managed to keep a couple of paces behind her without actually trotting.

We paused on the ground floor and caught our breath under the guise of inspecting the police seal on the door of the study where Fabian had been found. There really wasn't much to see and I realized that it was a very bad idea to stand here staring at it when I became aware of several sets of watching eyes somewhere behind us. Heaven knew what sinister motives were being imputed to us.

Evangeline glanced at me and I knew the back of her neck was crawling, too. Without a word, we returned to the staircase, climbing it to the next floor.

I felt limp as the door of our suite closed behind us. Evangeline looked as shaken as I felt.

'This is getting beyond a joke, Trixie.'

'If it was ever a joke, how come nobody was laughing?'

'I stand corrected.' But she slumped into a chair. 'See if Griselda is in her room.'

'No.' I looked, but she wasn't. 'She's probably off somewhere canoodling with Igor.'

'It's all right for *some*.' I couldn't tell whether Evangeline was bitter or just envious. 'There's too much canoodling going on, if you ask me.' Her face darkened. 'I blame Hugh. This is all his fault.'

'Hugh? He isn't even here. He's thousands of miles away.'

'Precisely! If he were here in England, attending to his own business, none of this would have happened.'

'Martha *is* his business now.'

Evangeline dismissed this with a gesture.

I took a deep breath, but the tap at the door saved us. I opened it and Meta came in with a tray.

'That's too heavy for you to carry up all those stairs.' I cleared a couple of magazines off the table so that she could set it down. 'Why didn't you have one of the minions bring it up?'

'It's all right.' She looked away and I knew that she couldn't have forced any of the minions to deliver anything to our suite. She was the only one brave enough to walk in on us—and she was looking a bit uncomfortable. 'Would you like anything else?'

'No, that's fine, thank you.' She couldn't wait to get away. She was through the door before I'd finished speaking.

'Our popularity grows by leaps and bounds.' Evangeline looked after her thoughtfully, then lifted one of the covers to reveal a symphony in green: a more than generous portion of spinach flan surrounded by a green salad.

'I'm glad she didn't use any tomatoes.' I lifted my own cover. 'I've seen enough red for today.'

'We all have. Although—' Evangeline frowned. 'I'm rather sorry we spoke so quickly about the wine. Perhaps we could have closed our eyes when we drank it.'

'We've still got the white wine,' I reminded her. 'In Job's fridge. He wouldn't mind if we went in and got it.'

'He might mind, but he wouldn't dare say so.' Evangeline's lips curved in a catlike smile. 'Especially if *I* go to collect it.'

'I'm coming, too. I want to check on Lora. That girl

132

worries me.' I replaced our serving covers and followed Evangeline into the hallway. 'She'll be the next into hospital if Job doesn't let her get some rest.'

'Job doesn't know the meaning of the word "rest"— for other people.'

'I suppose he's still at the hospital, waiting for the report on whether Fabian is going to make it.'

'More likely, he's trying to cadge some free medical samples for himself.' Evangeline gave the door of Job's suite a perfunctory tap before turning the knob.

'Lora?' I called softly, not wanting to startle her.

Silence. Except for the faint hum of machinery.

'She must have gone out.' Evangeline advanced into the sitting-room. 'Or else she didn't hear you. *That* wouldn't surprise me.'

'I don't want to startle her.' But I tried again, a bit louder. 'Lora? Lora?'

'Nobody home.' Not that it would have stopped her. She followed the humming sound to the small white refrigerator in the far corner. 'Ah, here we are . . .' She stooped to open it.

'WHAT ARE YOU DOING?' Lora stood in the doorway of one of the inner rooms. She was wild-eyed and dishevelled, as though she had just awakened from a nightmare. Or to a nightmare. 'GET AWAY FROM THERE!'

'It's all right, my dear.' Evangeline straightened up and stepped back. 'We've just come for our wine. You remember,' she added, as Lora showed no sign of comprehension. 'You very kindly offered to put our white wine in your fridge to chill. We decided we'd like some with our meal.'

'We called,' I apologized. 'You didn't answer. We didn't think anyone was here.'

'I was asleep.' Lora ran her hands through her hair, over her face, down to rest against her throat. 'God, I feel terrible!'

'You fainted earlier,' I reminded her. 'That takes a lot out of you.' So did the condition I suspected she was in.

'Oh God!' She shuddered. 'It's all coming back to me. It really happened, didn't it? I didn't dream it? No . . .' Her face changed, she looked strangely at the fridge. 'No, I couldn't have dreamed *that*.'

'It's terrible, but it may not be as bad as it looked.' With a glare, I defied Evangeline to repeat her prognosis for Fabian's injuries. 'I'm sure they have a very good hospital here and Fabian will be getting the best of care.'

'Fabian?' Lora looked at me blankly. 'Oh yes, that was awful, too.' Her gaze swung back to the fridge, she seemed mesmerized by it.

'We should be getting a report from someone at the hospital soon. Why don't you come back and have a drink with us while we wait?' Evangeline moved forward and stooped again to open the fridge.

'NO! DON'T!' Lora shrieked. 'I—I mean—' She fought for control. 'I'll get it for you.' She stepped forward and tried to jostle Evangeline out of the way.

She should have known better. Evangeline's curiosity was thoroughly aroused and wild horses weren't going to get her away from that fridge now.

'No, no, don't trouble yourself.' Evangeline hip-blocked her and bumped, sending her staggering backwards. 'I can manage.'

'No, please—' But it was too late. Evangeline had thrown open the refrigerator door and begun groping inside.

'Leave it to Job!' she grumbled. 'I suppose a fridge with a light is more expensive in this country.'

Lora had begun to sob quietly. I could feel the hairs rising on the back of my neck.

'Evangeline, be careful—'

'Here we are!' Evangeline straightened up with a bottle in her hand and contradicted herself. 'No, we're not. This is red—and it's only a half-bottle.'

'Ours is a cardboard box,' I reminded her. 'A three-litre box—'

'Why would Job keep red wine in the fridge?' Evangeline moved towards the light and tilted the bottle to read the label. There was something wrong about the bottle. In fact, everything. It was the wrong shape and the label was just a small white square.

'It isn't wine,' Lora sobbed. 'Oh, put it back before he comes in and catches us!'

' "Type AB Positive," ' Evangeline read out. She lowered the bottle and looked at me. Then we both looked at Lora.

'Just what does this mean?' Evangeline thundered in her most menacing Ethel Barrymore voice.

'I don't know.' Lora quailed before her. 'I don't know anything. He told me not to go near the fridge. He told me never to open it. But I didn't think it would matter if I sneaked your wine box into a corner. And I'm frightened. I'm so frightened.'

'I don't blame you.' Poor Lora—Bluebeard's girlfriend. No wonder she was looking so awful.

'And . . . and that's not all,' Lora moaned. 'There . . . there are two more bottles . . . frozen . . . and in the freezer compartment. I found them when I put your wine box in. I was looking for some ice. But that one—' She gestured wildly at the bottle Evangeline still held. '*That* one wasn't there before. It's new. It's . . . it's *fresh* blood!' Her eyes rolled up in their sockets and she crashed to the floor.

'Julian,' I said faintly. 'Where's Julian? I want Julian.'

'So do I. Why,' Evangeline asked fretfully, 'why is there never a policeman around when you need one?'

CHAPTER 15

'Another drop of brandy, Evangeline?' she inquired tenderly of herself. 'Why, thank you, Evangeline,' she answered, 'I don't mind if I do. It's the shock, you know. It isn't every day one discovers that an old colleague and friend is a ravening monster.'

'I'll drink to that!' I held my own glass out for a refill.

We had left the wine box in the fridge. Somehow the thought of it having been nestling there amid all that blood had caused us to lose any taste for white wine.

'It's funny . . .' I sipped reflectively. 'In the old movies, it was always the *actor* who went crackers after being trapped in a long run and had an identity crisis about his character. Too long playing *Othello* and he went home and strangled his wife or girlfriend—'

On the sofa, Lora twitched and moaned. We had decided we could never forgive ourselves if we left her in Job's suite and anything happened to her, so we had brought her back with us. Not that it was easy. We couldn't carry her, so we'd had to drag her by her heels. It meant that her head had thumped a bit, but it hadn't seemed to harm her—or even help her regain consciousness. We'd been nervous about the danger of being seen by the minions, who would have been sure to misinterpret our intentions if they caught us dragging an unconscious girl to our lair.

'She's still out.' Evangeline wandered over to check on her.

'Then there was the classic about the ventriloquist who became dominated by his murderous dummy.' I hadn't expected anything else. If dragging her down the corridor hadn't jolted Lora back to her senses, she was out for a long count. 'Then he went around killing people—'

'Nonsense! Look at Boris Karloff. He was for ever playing monsters and villains—yet the most sinister thing he ever did in real life was deadhead his roses.'

'I'm talking films, not real life—' For a moment, something caught and nagged at me, but was gone before I could catch it. 'Where it was always the actors who went mad, never the directors.'

'The directors are far more likely, I agree. In fact, I wouldn't give a plugged nickel for the sanity of half the directors I worked under in the 'thirties and 'forties.'

'You and me both. And it looks like we're knee-deep in it again.'

'Poor Job,' Evangeline sighed. 'I suppose it was all those years in B pictures. *When the Werewolf Howled, The Dripping Fangs, Blood on the Moon*, all that lot. They didn't do him any good—professionally or personally.'

'They might have—if he hadn't managed to lose so many stuntmen making them. You don't suppose . . . ?'

'You mean some sort of blood sacrifice?' She was right

136

there with me—and neither of us was happy there. 'That would mean—' She broke off as the door opened.

'Ah, you are here!' Of course, there was no reason why Griselda should have knocked. She was occupying the suite, too. Igor was right behind her; he beamed at us and bowed.

'Oh God! That's all we need!' Evangeline presented her back to them both and stalked over to the fireplace to lean her forehead against the mantelpiece.

Unfortunately, the wind chose that moment to gust again and a large puff of smoke billowed out and enveloped her. We could hear her coughing somewhere inside it.

'A nasty night, *hein?*' Griselda didn't bother to conceal her delight. '*Und* a nasty day, too. Haff ve had news from der hospital yet? Is Fabian still alive? *Und*—' she strolled over to stare down at Lora—'vot is wrong mit *dis* vun?'

'For God's sake!' Evangeline surfaced, spluttering and furious. 'Speak either English or German. Don't use that mongrel mix on us! *We're* not an audience!'

'Zo?' Griselda watched the soot settling on Evangeline's face and hair and smiled seraphically. She was in a suspiciously good mood, like a cat that had been at the cream—or the blood.

'Would you like some brandy?' I offered quickly, trying to blot out my own terrible thoughts.

'*Ja!*' 'How kind!' They both accepted enthusiastically and I went for the decanter, avoiding Evangeline's glaring fury.

Of course they settled themselves in chairs then and prepared to be sociable. The grinding of Evangeline's teeth was almost audible. On the sofa, Lora moaned softly and shifted position.

'Life is difficult for the young.' Igor glanced over at her sympathetically. 'They take everything so seriously.'

'Life is long,' Griselda agreed. 'Und so many opportunities present themselves for a second time . . .' She and Igor smiled at each other.

Evangeline snorted and stamped into the bathroom, slamming the door behind her.

Griselda smiled and shrugged, relishing Evangeline's discomfort. 'Such a temper!'

Lora moaned again and twisted restlessly. It looked as though she was regaining consciousness. Her hand fell away from her throat to trail on the carpet, her eyelids fluttered. Then the flurry of animation subsided, she went limp again. I began to wonder whether we should call a doctor. Surely it wasn't natural for a faint to last so long.

Igor's attention had been attracted. He rose and prowled over to the sofa, staring down at her with a frown.

'What is this?' He crouched over her, bending closer and closer to that exposed throat. When he looked up, there was a peculiar intensity in his eyes and his upper lip was drawn back, almost in a snarl. I wouldn't have been surprised to see fangs descend. 'When did this wound happen?'

'Several days ago. She *claimed* one of the bats bit her.' I gave myself a mental shake. Did she have that injury before the bats started flying around? 'The way she keeps picking at it, it will never heal. She never gives it a chance.'

'You believe, do you, that that is the reason the wound will not heal? The reason it remains so fresh, so ... tempting?'

'Why not? Do you have a better theory?' I didn't really want to hear it. On the other hand, I wanted to be reassured that it wasn't just me, that someone else could have the nightmare vision I kept trying to deny.

'I have seen such things before,' Igor brooded. 'In Transylvania ... where the old ways still linger.'

'Igor—' Griselda spoke warningly. 'It is no concern of ours.'

'The old insanities, you mean!' Evangeline snapped, re-emerging into the room. She must have been standing in the doorway listening.

'Many have disbelieved.' Igor shrugged. 'Many more have jested. It changes nothing.'

'I assure you, some things *can* be changed.' Evangeline crossed the room purposefully. I saw that she was carrying a glass of water. Ice-cold water, I'd bet.

'What are you going to do with that?' Griselda obligingly fed her a cue.

'In the absence of smelling salts,' Evangeline said, 'this has been known to work wonders.'

Lora's eyelashes fluttered again. Rather nervously, I thought.

'If we wanted to stay in period character,' I suggested, 'it ought to be burning feathers under her nose. Of course, that might be kind of dangerous.' Yes, there was a definite nervous reaction. Interesting. I wondered how long Lora had been conscious.

'Since no cameras are turning at the moment—' Evangeline advanced inexorably. 'I think we'll make do with this.'

'So practical,' Griselda murmured, for once approving.

'You'd better stand back, Igor,' Evangeline directed brisky.

'Yes, yes.' He moved away hastily—and noisily. There was amusement in his face. He, too, had noticed the twitching eyelids.

'One school of thought favours the few drops at a time method—' Evangeline suited action to the words, dribbling water on to Lora's face. 'But, personally, I prefer the whole glass at a time method. With refills, if necessary.'

'Oooooh . . .' It wasn't necessary. Lora's eyelids flew open. She tried to mask the dislike in her eyes. 'Oooh . . . where am I? What . . . what happened?'

'You fainted, dear,' I said.

'Passed out,' Evangeline corrected, not willing to let her get away with anything so ladylike as a faint. 'You'll be all right now.' She still held the glass tilted threateningly above Lora's face.

'Oooooh . . .' Defensively, Lora struggled into a sitting position. 'I feel terrible.'

'Poor dear.' I wasn't surprised. She must have been genuinely unconscious to begin with or she'd never have let us drag her down the corridor the way we had. She'd have a few bruises to show for that but, with any luck, might never find out how she got them.

139

But bruises weren't all Lora had to worry about right now. I tried not to stare at the raw red marks on her throat.

'You might as well drink the rest of it.' Evangeline thrust the glass of water at her. 'Then we'll give you some brandy.'

'I don't want—' Lora broke off and drank the three-quarters of a glass of water in one continuous swallow. Yes, the original faint had been genuine.

'Thanks,' she said weakly, handing the glass back to Evangeline, who stared at it unbelievingly.

'That's better,' I said quickly, before Evangeline could ask her who had been her servant last week. 'Now just lean back and take it easy. You don't want to rush—'

The loud knock at the door startled us all. I went to open the door, but no one was waiting for niceties like that. The door burst open and Julian charged into the room, nearly knocking me down. Gwenda was right behind him. Meta, moving more slowly, was the last to enter; she closed the door behind her and leaned against it, looking at us thoughtfully.

'It's about time!' Evangeline glared at Julian. 'Where have you been all day?'

'With the police, first.' Ignoring her fury, he put an arm protectively around her shoulders. 'Then we all went back to *Yesterday's Dreams* and helped Griff clean up.'

'We saw your dummy—' Gwenda circled Evangeline, inspecting her closely, making sure she was all right. 'With the knife in its back. Oh, it was howwid . . . horrid! I'm so glad you're all right. You *are* all right?'

'I'm fine.' Impatiently, Evangeline shook off Julian's arm.

'And there's nothing you want to tell me?' Julian asked, an insinuating note in his voice.

'Tell?' Evangeline gave him the blank innocent stare. There was plenty we wanted to tell him—but not in front of so many witnesses. 'What on earth could we have to tell you?'

'That's what I'd like to know,' Julian said. 'I had a report about you as soon as I got in. Someone said they'd seen you trying to dispose of a body.'

'Body? Oh . . .' Evangeline did the puzzled look dissolv-

140

ing into amused comprehension. 'That was no body—that was Lora. She took one of her little turns and we . . . helped her back here to lie down.'

'I see.' Julian had the jaundiced look that told Evangeline she wasn't getting away with a thing—and neither was I. We already had form for this sort of behaviour. 'And you're better now, Lora?'

'Oh! Oh yes . . .' As though startled at being so abruptly addressed, Lora let her hand flutter up to clutch at her throat. While it was there, it pulled at the collar of her dress, inching it higher to hide the marks on her throat. 'It was just a . . . a temporary weakness. I'm fine now.' She began to struggle to her feet. 'I ought to get back to my room now. Job will be looking for me.'

'Job's not back yet,' Meta said.

'Oh!' There was no mistaking the look of relief on Lora's face. 'But I ought to get back just the same.'

'I don't think that's wise,' Evangeline said. 'You're still not very strong. I think it might be best if you stayed somewhere else tonight. Perhaps Gwenda and Meta can fit a cot into their room for you. Then, if you feel ill in the night, they can look after you. Job would be no use at all in a crisis.'

'Wight—right!' Gwenda was game, if a little disconcerted at having her living arrangements redesigned so abruptly.

'Oh, but—' Lora was torn between relief and apprehension. 'When Job comes back and finds I'm not there—'

'We'll explain to him,' I said firmly. 'In fact, if we hint that you might have developed something contagious, he'll be delighted you're not there.' One could always rely on Job's hypochondria.

'Well, if you're sure you don't mind . . . ?' Lora appealed to Gwenda. 'I *could* use a good night's sleep. I mean, Job usually has a script conference going in the sitting-room until the small hours.'

'Umm-hmm.' We knew what she meant. 'You just go along with Gwenda, dear. You'll feel much better in the morning.'

Meta swung the door open, looking as though she didn't

141

believe one word anybody had been saying. Griselda and Igor stayed where they were, giving every appearance of interested spectators at a play especially performed for their benefit. I half-expected them to begin applauding.

'Yes . . .' Lora swayed as she rose to her feet and I moved in to support her on one side.

To my surprise, Evangeline came forward to support her on the other. Of course, it was a lot easier now that she was on her feet and capable of noving. I realized that Evangeline intended this as a demonstration of the way we had originally helped Lora back to our suite, thus giving the lie to whatever the minions might have reported.

Gwenda and Julian fell in behind us. Meta closed the door—firmly discouraging Griselda and Igor from coming along too—and followed us. She had the look of someone mentally running through her CV wondering if she could land a better job. At this point, *any* other job must seem an improvement to her.

There was a rustling and scampering of human mice as we proceeded down the corridor to the back staircase. The minions were keeping out of our way, but they wanted to see what was going on.

There wasn't much to see. Lora was more or less moving under her own steam now, but wouldn't win any Miss Health-and-Fitness Contest. Evangeline kept a firm grip on her elbow and I was still half-supporting her with an arm around her waist. Julian was close behind, ready to catch her if she fell. Gwenda and Meta trailed us, murmuring to each other in worried tones.

The light was dimmer at the end of the hallway. So dim that it took me a moment to realize that what I had thought was a window alcove was, in fact, a recessed mirror with a semi-circular table below it. A lovely, but somehow jarring, flower arrangement stood on the table, reflected in the mirror. Vaguely aware of something wrong, I studied the arrangement. They must be artificial flowers; most of them were out-of-season and sprinkled among them were a few weird blooms I had never seen before. But why should that disturb me so . . . ?

Someone screamed. One of the minions, unwarily descending the stairs, had turned the corner and come upon us unexpectedly. And screamed. Not one of those minions had a nerve left in their bodies—or a brain in their heads.

'Look!' The minion shrieked, pointing to the mirror. 'Look!'

I looked automatically. There was nothing to see. I began to turn back to the minion, then did a double-take as the realization struck me. Literally, there was nothing to see.

Lora was standing directly in front of the mirror—but she was not reflected in it. The soft grey depths of the mirror showed only the flower arrangement and the blank wall opposite. But not Lora.

'Vampires . . .' the minion wailed. 'Vampires cast no shadows . . . and no reflections.'

'Move, Trixie!' Evangeline gave me a shove and we pulled Lora away from the mirror.

'Keep moving!'

The minion flattened herself against the wall and scuttled along it crabwise as we bore down on the stairs. I was aware of Julian reaching out and grabbing the minion's arm, pulling her into our orbit, stopping her from running to the others and spreading alarm.

I was alarmed enough for everyone. As we hustled Lora away from the mirror, a further terrifying realization had hit me.

Lora had cast no reflection in that mirror. And neither had we!

CHAPTER 16

'Where did that mirror come from?' Meta spoke with suppressed fury. 'I've never seen it before!'

'I don't know,' Gwenda said. 'It wasn't here this morning.'

143

'Help me move it.' Meta reached for one side of the ornate frame. 'It's blocking the window.'

Evangeline continued propelling Lora up the stairs. They were doing just fine on their own, so I dropped back and left them to it. I wanted to see what was going on here.

'I'll do that!' So did Julian. 'Here, hang on to her.' He thrust the hapless minion at Gwenda and strode forward to the mirror.

He wasn't reflected in it either. It lived in a timeless world of its own, perpetually reflecting a gleaming semi-circle of polished wood and an exotic flower arrangement with blankness all around it.

Julian wrenched the mirror from its perch atop the table, revealing the recessed curtained window behind it. I breathed more easily. I had been right about the window after all.

The minion squawked as Julian swung the mirror to the floor. It was facing her—and neither she nor Gwenda were reflected in it.

'I want to go home,' she sobbed, fighting to escape Gwenda's iron grip. 'All the way home—to Surbiton!'

No trace of their struggle appeared in the untroubled grey depths of the mirror. It continued to show only the table top and floral arrangement now well out of its range.

I moved closer to inspect this interesting phenomenon.

'Here we are.' Julian swivelled it round to display the accession label pasted on the back:

No. 245 YESTERDAY'S DREAMS
I Waltzed With A Vampire
Anvil Productions, 1956.
12/10/89

'That Griff!' Meta raged. 'I'll kill him!'

'I don't know.' I kicked off my shoes and slumped into an armchair. 'I suppose you couldn't really turn into a vampire without knowing that something was going on, but it had me worried for a few minutes there. I mean, look at all the filthy concoctions Job has ordered served up to us in the canteen—suppose he found some way of sneaking *real* blood into them and it wasn't all tomato paste?'

'That wouldn't necessarily turn us into vampires.' Nevertheless, Evangeline was more shaken than she cared to admit. She poured brandy with a reckless hand. 'Besides, who should he want to do that?'

'If he's crazy, does he need a reason? I mean, what is he *doing* with all that blood?'

All that blood. The vision of those bottles in the fridge rose up in our minds. We were trapped in this clifftop prison with a madman in command. Simultaneously we shuddered and gulped at our brandy.

'Just how crazy do you suppose he is?' I persisted. We had to face this. 'Do you think he's dangerous—really dangerous?'

'Well, he certainly hasn't done Fabian any good.'

'You think *he* did that? But why?'

'Why not?' Evangeline shrugged and continued reflectively, 'Perhaps because he's no longer getting enough . . . sustenance . . . from Lora.'

'Oh no!' I closed my eyes, but I couldn't close my mind. Again I saw those raw red unhealing wounds on Lora's throat. Lora—who was Job's constant companion. Lora—who was with him day . . . and night. Lora, who was growing visibly weaker and frailer with each passing day—while Job, despite his age and crushing workload, was flourishing.

'Job has been draining the energy and creativity of his associates for decades,' Evangeline said. 'It may have seemed just a small additional step for him to graduate to draining their actual lifeblood.'

'I can't believe it—it's too horrible!' But the same wounds Lora bore had been apparent deep in Fabian's neck. 'I can't believe it . . . but it happened.'

'Even worse,' Evangeline reminded me. 'At least half of the minions suspect *us* of being responsible.'

'They seemed to be *prepared* to suspect us.' I remembered something else. 'I found garlic outside our door before anything even happened. We'd hardly arrived.'

'So someone had been spreading their poison in advance. That doesn't surprise me. Job always did try to shift the blame for his peccadilloes on to others.'

'I'd call it something stronger than a peccadillo—'

The sudden knock at the door startled us both. The way I jumped, I would have spilled my drink—if there had been anything left to spill.

'Why, hello—' Evangeline looked over my head as the door opened. Her eyes widened. 'Come in, Job. We were just talking about you.'

'Talk of the devil—' I broke off. For once, the cliché was too apt—and possibly too accurate.

'Hello, girls.' Job didn't notice. 'You got any more of that brandy going?'

'Coming right up.' Evangeline was heading for the decanter anyway.

'Jeez!' Job dropped down on the sofa and buried his face in his hands. 'I don't want to go through anything like that again in a hurry.'

'Fabian?' I hardly needed to ask.

'Dead on arrival,' Job confirmed. 'Did you doubt it for a minute?'

'Not really.' I found that I hadn't. 'But the way the medics kept working over him, I hoped . . .'

'Not a chance. We were just trying to keep the others from panicking. It was a pretty gruesome sight. Oh—' He looked up and accepted his drink from Evangeline. 'Thanks, sweetheart.'

'Have you been at the hospital all this time?' Evangeline asked.

'Where else?'

Evangeline and I exchanged glances. He'd had time for a quick nap in his coffin. True, it was still daylight outside, but in this climate no self-respecting vampire needed to worry about the odd ray of sunlight flickering through the fog to wreak havoc with his system. No wonder Dracula had felt right at home landing here, the conditions were probably better than they had been in Transylvania.

Transylvania . . . Another thought slid through my

146

mind, chilling my blood. Igor had spent a lot of time in Transylvania; long enough to be conversant with its customs. It was Igor who had dared to put into words the uneasy suspicions we had begun to harbour about Lora's wounds. Igor had described the wound as 'tempting'. Where was Igor right now? And Griselda had been spending all her spare time with him—was she safe?

I shook myself mentally. Grisly was tough enough to take care of herself—tough enough to *be* a vampire herself. Maybe that was why she and Igor got on so well. And what was Igor doing here in the first place? He and Job were an unlikely pair to seek each other out—unless they had more in common than we realized. Had they met at some sort of Vampires' Convention?

Recognizing that I was off in some reverie of my own, Evangeline kicked me, none too subtly. I blinked and sat up straighter, trying to look alert. Was I in danger of missing something important?

'The irony is that it's mostly Fabian's own fault that he died like that,' Job was saying. 'In the ordinary way, I'd have had cameras and lighting all set up in there and waiting. There'd have been a crew on hand ready to start shooting as soon as Fabian showed up. But you saw the way he was carrying on lately. Lora warned me that he was about ready to try his old trick of walking out again. Not that she needed to. I could see that for myself. So I wasn't wasting anybody's time until Fabian actually showed—then *he* could hang around and cool his heels while the crew set up the scene. That would show him! Don't worry, he'd get the message all right. In a way—' Job sighed heavily—'you could say Fabian was his own worst enemy.'

'Demonstrably not.' Evangeline slanted an oblique look at Job. That was *his* story. It was equally possible that Job had deliberately neglected to order the scene prepared so that he could lure Fabian on to the empty set and attack him without fear of being disturbed. He could then . . . deal . . . with Fabian at his leisure and leave the body on the set, knowing that it would not be disturbed until he gave the order to prepare for the scene in the study. Until it was too late for anyone to help Fabian.

'Yeah,' Job sighed again. 'I suppose you're right.'

I jumped involuntarily, then realized that he was referring to Evangeline's last remark and not to my secret thoughts. Thank goodness he couldn't read minds—or I might be next on the menu.

'And *I* suppose the police will be back here in the morning.' Evangline was getting back on form. I noticed she kept more than arm's length from Job, however. There was no sense in taking chances.

'They did mutter something about that,' Job admitted. 'But those accents!' He shook his head. 'I gotta admit, I still can't understand half of what some of these guys are saying. But I guess that was the gist of it.'

'I should think so.' Evangeline eyed him coldly and I began to fear what she might say next.

'How far along with the film are we, Job?' I asked quickly. 'Can we finish it without Fabian?'

'I dunno.' Job seemed to look deep within himself. 'It will be tricky, but I think maybe we can manage it.'

'I'm sure you can,' Evangeline purred. After all, he wouldn't have risked killing Fabian unless the film was more or less in the can.

'Because . . . I was thinking—' I went on, even more quickly. 'If you needed any more cover shots, long shots—anything but actual close-ups . . .'

'Yeah?' Job encouraged me, a note of interest in his voice.

'Well, do you remember Des? You met him back at our lodgings in St John's Wood. Tallish, darkish, rather handsome—and he plays the clarinet?'

'Ye-eah . . .' Job pondered a moment. 'I guess there is kind of a resemblance at that. Good enough for long shots with the right make-up. Ye-eah, Trixie, sweetheart, I think you've come up with a definite possibility. Clarinet, huh? Maybe he could double on some background music, too.'

'I'm sure he could. He's awfully good.' I had been haunted by guilt every time I remembered Des's gallant smile as he waved the rest of us off on our journey to

Whitby. But I had only been able to wangle a part for Gwenda in the production until this opportunity presented itself.

If you could call it an opportunity. I was so pleased with myself for a moment that I forgot I might be throwing Des into danger.

'Can you get in touch with him? Get him up here fast?'

'Well, I don't know what his other commitments are right now . . .' Suddenly I was hedging, wondering whether I'd be doing Des such a favour after all.

'Try! Can you call him tonight?' As usual, a show of reluctance was sharpening Job's interest. 'Offer him— Well, let me talk to him after he's talked to you. You explain to him what a good deal it is, then I'll sort out the minor details.'

'It's a bit late tonight.' Job's reference to payment as a minor detail increased my reluctance. 'Maybe we should wait until morning.' And maybe, after I'd slept on it, I could decide whether it was a good idea or not.

'Nonsense!' Evangeline had no doubt about the idea. I could see that she was thinking in terms of reinforcements. 'I'll call him myself, if Trixie doesn't feel up to it. We'll get him here.'

'Great! Swell!' But Job was still preoccupied by other considerations. Suddenly he was looking wearier, his vitality dimmed. 'I don't know,' he sighed. 'Who needs all this hassle? Why did somebody have to kill that bastard right in the middle of the picture? Why couldn't they have waited until we were into the post-production stage?'

Maybe because Fabian wouldn't be around then. He'd have done his work and departed. Or maybe because Job could use the inconvenience of it all as an argument to prove his innocence. ('*Me? Kill an actor before the picture was finished? I'd be cutting my own throat.*') Abruptly, I wished I hadn't thought of that.

'Who do you think might have done it?' Evangeline was eyeing Job sardonically. 'Who hates you as much as they hated Fabian?'

'Hate *me?*' The idea galvanized Job into animation. He

149

sprang to his feet. 'Nobody hates me! Why should anybody hate me? What did I ever do to anybody?'

'*Methinks*—' Evangeline dropped her voice to its lowest register. She sounded more like John than Ethel Barrymore now. '*Methinks the gentleman doth protest too much.*'

'Now you cut that out!' Job glared at her. 'I don't want to hear anything more like that!' He drained off what remained of his brandy in a gulp and looked at the glass in dissatisfaction.

Pointedly, Evangeline made no move to refill it. The silence lengthened.

'You girls are looking tired tonight,' Job said. 'I guess it's been a rough day on everybody, huh?'

'Roughest on Fabian,' Evangeline said. 'But, yes, we *are* rather tired.'

'Yeah.' Job was becoming uncomfortable. 'Well, I suppose I better let you get your beauty sleep. Besides—' He set the empty glass down on the table. 'I'm thirsty. This kinda stuff is no good for a real thirst. I've got some low-cal drink in my fridge. I'll go have some of that. Want any?'

Our mouths fell open. We shook our heads vehemently and went on shaking them.

'Suit yourselves. You won't forget that telephone call, will you?' Job stared at us strangely. We must have looked like Harpo Marx in duplicate. 'Get some sleep, then. I'll see you in the morning.' He looked back over his shoulder nervously as he closed the door behind him.

'I never thought about it before—' At last Evangeline found her voice. Mine was still missing. 'But I suppose there *aren't* many calories in blood!'

In the morning, the only brightness was the thought that Des was on his way up here. I hoped I had done the right thing in mentioning him to Job, but it was too late to do anything about it now. Anything but worry—and there were plenty of other things to worry about that were more immediate.

Lora still looked terrible. Of course, one night away from Job couldn't be expected to restore her to health—it was a step in the right direction, that was all. If she was smart, she would find an excuse to keep well away from Job, but I was afraid that her ambition—or perhaps her greed—outweighed her intelligence. She was already back at Job's side, taking notes about something he had decided he wanted done.

Mrs Bright looked even worse than Lora. She was wearing black and her knitting-bag hung from her arm disregarded as she stared into space, occasionally shaking her head in denial. One more nervous breakdown in the making.

In contrast, Alanna was one of the most cheerful people on the set—except when she looked at her mother. Then an anxious frown marred her perfection and she seemed older than her years. Until she looked at Barney. Unfortunately, Barney was too busy to do much in the way of responding. He sent her a few abstracted smiles, but Job was keeping him fully stretched—and then some.

'Barney! Julian! Hobie!' Job bellowed. 'Come on! Script conference!' They all huddled briefly, then went downstairs to the canteen, where they'd have copious supplies of coffee on hand. Lora went with them, flourishing her notebook as a badge of office, ready to work herself to death. Or maybe a fate worse than death. You just can't tell some people anything.

The minions darted about like silverfish. By this time, they were even afraid of each other. They were inventing bits of work to keep themselves busy; they spoke together in hurried conferences; but all the while they kept one eye on their line of exit, ready to run for it if a fellow conferee made a menacing move.

We were all waiting for the police to arrive, but they were taking their time about it. Perhaps they moved more slowly up here, or perhaps it was part of a war of nerves. More prosaically, perhaps they were just waiting for an autopsy report so that they'd have a better idea of the questions they wanted to ask.

Evangeline was sitting in a corner, idly gossiping with Koji, who was tenderly polishing some of his lenses and

151

filters. He nodded agreement as Evangeline spoke and even chuckled softly. He was the only relaxed person in the vicinity. I started over to join them; if there were any chuckles going round, I wanted in on them.

'Oh, Miss Dolan, Trixie—' Mrs Bright blocked my way. 'If I could just speak to you for a moment . . . ?'

'Of course.' There was no 'of course' about it. I no more wanted to have a cosy conversation with her than I wanted to drink anything out of Job's refrigerator, but you had to be polite.

'In private, I mean.' She looked around nervously. 'Over here.' She led the way to the alcove by the snuggery. I saw Evangeline signal to me that she was going up to our suite and shrugged my shoulders at her. Koji chuckled again.

'There.' Mrs Bright settled herself so that her back was to the wall and she had a full view of the surrounding area. Her eyes were rolling wildly and I hoped she wasn't going to have some kind of fit there and then. She looked even worse now that I could see her clearly. That black dress did nothing for her, but it flaunted her mourning status, which was what she intended. It was a wonder she hadn't strewn a few ashes over it, there were enough around.

Having got me into a corner, she seemed in no hurry to have that conversation. I smiled at her encouragingly, hoping she would stop hyperventilating soon. For a woman her size, she had suddenly grown gaunt and haggard. Judging by the dark circles under her eyes, she had had little or no sleep last night. And this was the longest length of time I had ever seen her go without knitting. No wonder Alanna was so worried. I was getting worried myself.

'Well, here we are.' I smiled at her again.

'Yes . . .' she breathed, her brooding gaze scanning the room beyond the alcove.

'*You* wanted to talk to *me*.' Perhaps she had forgotten that already. I didn't get the impression that she was connecting very well.

'Yes. Oh yes . . .' She wasn't even looking at me. Then suddenly she shuddered and turned and gave me her full attention.

152

I could have done without it. Abruptly, I felt like a butterfly being pinned to a cork board. The intensity of her gaze pierced through me. She leaned closer and I shrank back involuntarily.

'Trixie, the police are coming back, aren't they?'

'I should think so. I'm surprised they're not here now.'

'Yes . . .' It was not the answer she wanted to hear, but it was the one she had expected. 'It's terrible, terrible! I don't see why they can't leave us alone . . . with our grief.'

'It is a murder case.' She was also the only one grieving, but it wouldn't be tactful to point that out. 'It's their job.'

'Yes . . .' That didn't satisfy her either. 'I don't see why they can't let us handle it by ourselves. Julian is a police-man. I'm sure he's perfectly capable of dealing with the situation—*and* he'd be discreet.'

'Julian is a London policeman. He doesn't have any juris-diction up here.'

'I don't see why not.' She was being wilfully obtuse. 'A policeman is a policeman, isn't he? What difference do a few miles make?'

'You'd have to take that up with the Whitby police.' And the best of British luck to her if she tried it!

'The Whitby police!' Terror flared in her eyes. You'd think the entire constabulary was composed of Draculas. 'Do you . . . do you think they're going to . . . to search the place?'

'Vhy should you ask zhat?' I had not been aware of Griselda's approach. Now she stood before us, head raised high, nostrils flaring, accent so thick I barely understood what she was saying. *The Baroness at Bay* had been her first Hollywood film; she had used the same stance in that— and I understood they'd had to dub her voice for most of the picture because of that accent.

Mrs Bright gave a small shriek before regaining control of her nerves. She hadn't seen Griselda approaching either.

'You said zhe police, zhey vill search—' Griselda advanced menacingly. 'Vhere did you get zhis information? Vhen vill zhey arrive?'

'I . . . I don't know.' Mrs Bright watched her warily. 'I was asking Trixie.'

'*You* have zhis information?' Grisly glared at me, her hands twitched as though she would grab me and shake it out of me. 'You vill tell me! I must know!'

'I don't know any more than you do,' I disclaimed hastily. 'The police are bound to come back sooner or later—this is a murder investigation. And I wouldn't be surprised if they did some searching. They'll want to find the murder weapon, after all.' I decided not to mention that I thought an orthodontist would have a better chance of discovering the weapon than the police.

'Oh!' Mrs Bright went even paler. Perhaps she had a few suspicions of her own. 'Oh, this is terrible! I wish I'd never let Alanna sign that dreadful contract. There's been nothing but trouble on this picture.' Her eyes filled with tears. 'And now we've lost dear Fabian and the police haven't the decency to leave us alone with our grief!'

'Very sad,' Griselda said dismissively. She frowned at me. 'You are sure you do not know vhen zhey vill arrive?'

'They don't have to make appointments, you know. They just show up—as and when it suits *their* convenience.'

'*Ja*. Zhat iss so.' Grisly had been in enough Midnight-Knock-on-the-Door dramas to recognize the truth in this. Her eyes grew thoughtful. 'I must speak to Igor. I vill see you later.' She was gone as abruptly as she had arrived.

'Oh, this is awful, awful,' Mrs Bright moaned.

'It isn't very pleasant for any of us!' I was prepared to be sympathetic, but my sympathy was wearing thin. Besides, Mrs Bright was feeling so sorry for herself that anyone else's sympathy was redundant.

'Look—' I took a deep breath and tried again. 'You mustn't go on brooding about this, you'll make yourself ill. Why don't you go and find yourself a quiet corner and . . . and knit something?'

'How could you?' She reacted as though I had said what I really wanted to say. 'How could you be so cruel? So callous? I was knitting a scarf for dear Fabian!'

'I'm sorry. I didn't mean to—'

'Oh no, of course you didn't mean to. None of you ever mean to. You just don't think. You never consider my feelings at all!'

I can tell when I'm on the receiving end of a broadside meant for somebody else. This speech should have been aimed at Alanna, but she was nowhere in sight. I only wished I wasn't.

'You laugh at my knitting, I know, but if you had nerves like mine, *you'd* do anything that soothed them.'

'I'm sure I would,' I babbled placatingly. 'The atmosphere is so unsettling around here—'

'All right, then!' She thrust the knitting-bag into my hands. '*You* knit something!'

Before I could protest, she had turned and darted away—leaving me holding the bag.

CHAPTER 17

'What on earth do you have there?' Evangeline demanded crossly as I returned to the suite shortly afterwards.

'Mrs Bright's knitting-bag. I can't find Alanna or I'd have given it to her, and Mrs Bright has disappeared, so I thought I'd dump it here until I can get it back to them. I certainly don't want it.'

'Disappeared?' Evangeline looked hopeful. 'You mean she's gone? For good?'

'I doubt that. She took umbrage at something I said and practically threw the bag at me and charged off.'

'That sounds most unlike her. I've never known her to let that bag out of her hands.' Evangeline eyed it speculatively. 'I wonder what she keeps in it—besides her knitting, that is.'

'I don't know and I don't care. *Evangeline!*' She had torn the bag from my grasp. 'You can't *do* that!'

'Nonsense!' Evangeline upended the bag over the table. Yarn and steel needles slid out on to the smooth surface with a clatter. 'If she doesn't care enough about it to hang on to it . . .' She leaned over the tangled heap, inspecting it closely.

'She just lost her temper,' I said. 'I'm sure she didn't intend to *give* it to me. I upset her and that was all she had to throw.'

'*How* did you upset her?' Evangeline had tilted the empty bag towards the light and was peering into it. 'What did you say?'

'Nothing much. She must have been looking for a fight. She's still shattered about Fabian and furious with Alanna. I just got in the way and she dumped everything on me.'

'Including her knitting?' Evangeline was turning the bag carefully now, scrutinizing the outside. 'There *has* to be more to it than that. What *exactly* did you say to her?'

'I can't remember exactly, it all went so fast. I think I told her to go away and knit something.'

'Interesting . . . usually, you can't *stop* her from knitting. But, now that I come to think of it, I haven't seen those needles in her hand since Fabian died.'

'Neither have I—' We both looked at the assortment of glittering needles in their nest of yarn. Was it my imagination, or was the tip of one of them not glittering in the lamplight as brightly as the others?

Evangeline spotted it at the same moment. She swooped and caught up the tangled mass, holding it close to her eyes and then cautiously disentangling one of the long thin steel needles. A loop of yarn slid off of it and several stitches unravelled.

'I believe we've found the murder weapon, Trixie—and fangs had nothing to do with it.'

We stared at the sharp tip, dimmed by flecks of what might have been rust. But you don't get rust on stainless steel.

'*That's* what we were talking about!' I remembered suddenly. 'She wanted to know whether the police were going to search the house. After I said I expected they'd have to, she went and picked that fight with me.'

'The Queen of the Dirty Tricks Department—we should have remembered her reputation earlier. She's noted for nasty tricks. And now she's killed Fabian and fixed it so that the murder weapon will be found in your possession. She's foisted the evidence on you!'

'Not for long she hasn't!' I reached for the knitting-bag. 'I'm going to take it back and stuff it down her throat!'

'Temper, temper, Trixie! That may be just what she wants. If she can provide witnesses to testify that you have violent tendencies, she's more than half way to framing you for the whole thing.'

'You're right.' My temper cooled as rapidly as it had flared. (No wonder I had never been able to make it as a redhead.) 'So what do we do now?'

'Ordinarily, I would suggest that we find Julian and give the evidence to him, but I fear the dear misguided boy would simply hand it over to the local police—and I do not feel that they would take us seriously.'

She meant that they wouldn't let her grab centre stage and stay there. They'd take away the evidence and shuffle her off to the sidelines. Worse, they might not consider it evidence at all.

'But why should Mrs Bright want to kill Fabian? She wanted him to marry Alanna. Now, if she'd killed Barney, I could undertand it. Barney was ruining all her plans.'

'I wonder . . .' Evangeline assumed that faraway expression she had used in *The Happy Couple* series to signal that all the clues were beginning to make sense at last. Instinctively, I mistrusted it.

'I wonder if Our Madame Defarge was really as upset as she pretended to be over Alanna's attraction to Barney. After all, it left the field clear for her.'

'You can't mean it!' I gasped. Even for Evangeline, this was going too far. 'Fabian *has* to be at least thirty years younger than she is. Besides, he couldn't stand her.'

'I never suggested that her feelings were reciprocated. But you must admit that it was obvious that she was mad about the boy.'

'It was also obvious that he was going to put her on a one-way boat to China just as soon as he got the ring on Alanna's finger.'

'Exactly! So Madame Defarge, a woman scorned, had a double motive for killing him. He was plotting to remove Alanna from her influence *and* he spurned her own advances to him. Men have been killed for far less.'

'Maybe. But I don't think you'd better try to have it both ways. It has to be one or the other.'

'I don't see why.' Evangeline twiddled the knitting needle crossly. Nasty glints of light radiated from the long shank.

'Because the police might believe *one* motive, but two like that would be laughed out of court.'

'The police . . .' Evangeline stared pensively at the tip of the needle. 'What a pity we aren't down in London with our sweet Superintendent Heydey. *He* would have understood.'

He would probably have had both of us in jail by this time—just on general principles. Evangeline's recollection of events is highly selective; she forgets any scene in which she does not feature to her advantage.

'Perhaps it *would* weaken the case to bring up the question of where Alanna's loyalties might lie if it came to a choice between her mother and her husband. We must concentrate on our stronger case: this was obviously a Crime of Passion. Madame Defarge threw herself at the young man's—'

'EVANGELINE!'

'Head, I was about to say.' She gave me an injured look. 'He spurned her, insulted her, laughed at her. So, in the heat of the moment, she hit out at him with the only weapon she had in her possession—a knitting needle. A long, sharp, steel knitting needle.'

'She might not have intended to kill him—' Against my better judgement, I augmented her fantasy. 'She only wanted to hurt him as he had hurt her—'

'Or blind him!' Evangeline said, with too much relish. 'And then she could devote the rest of her life to him, nursing him in remorse—'

'But she missed and hit an artery—' Suddenly, my voice and my certainty began to falter. This scenario was beginning to seem eerily familiar. Could I have seen it in a movie?

'Yes!' Evangeline had no such doubts. 'His career would have been ended; he would have been completely in her

158

power. She might have lost control over Alanna, but she would still have someone to dominate.'

'Except that he hated her and he had family who would take care of him. He wouldn't have needed to rely on Mrs Bright.' Common sense was creeping back into this discussion. Evangeline felt it and shook her shoulders impatiently.

'That's just the sort of argument the police would use,' she complained. 'That's why we must take care of this ourselves.'

'Oh yeah? Like how?'

'*We* know she's guilty, so we don't have to waste our time on any other suspects. We can concentrate on her until we've proved incontrovertibly she's guilty. Then we can present the whole case to the police.'

I wished she'd leave me out of these schemes of hers. I opened my mouth to say so, but she was already rushing ahead.

'There was so much blood. She couldn't have killed him without getting splashed with blood. All we have to do is find the bloodstained clothing.'

'Oh, is that all? You don't think she might have already burned it in her fireplace?'

'In that case, the police forensic experts will have to sift the ashes and do laboratory tests on them. That's the drawback of living in a place with an open fire in every room.

'Of course—' Evangeline brightened—'she might have removed all her clothes first. I understand that's a favourite method with axe murderers.'

'That would mean that she knew she was going to kill him.'

'Not necessarily. She might have been . . . offering herself to him. In place of Alanna.'

'Great! That would sure explain Fabian's repulsing her so fast and so insultingly. I can't imagine anything more horrible to a man than a naked mother-in-law bearing down on him with lustful intent. But I can't believe that even Mrs Bright would be so intensitive that she'd strip off without some sort of encouragement. I think we'd better go back to the bloodstained clothing—which we'll never find with all these fireplaces.'

'Fireplaces . . .' Evangeline sighed heavily. 'They may be picturesque, but they're far too convenient for villainy. I don't know what Job was thinking of.'

'And how about Job? He's going around with a fridge loaded with bottles of blood. Where did he get all that blood—if it wasn't from Fabian?'

'I hadn't forgotten that.' But I knew that, however momentarily, she had. 'Perhaps he was in league with Mrs Bright. Or perhaps he discovered the body soon afterward—while the blood was still pumping—and collected what he wanted . . . needed . . .' She let her voice trail away; the picture she was presenting was too unthinkable.

'Oh, the police will love *that* one. It's even better than a lust-crazed Madame Defarge assaulting Fabian's . . . honour.'

There was a long pause while she absorbed this. I waited for either a tantrum or an announcement that she was about to have one of her headaches—the headache was quieter—but she surprised me.

'You're right, Trixie. At this stage, we cannot rule either of them out. We must find more evidence.'

'Oh?' I didn't like the sound of this. 'And how do you propose that we do that?'

'We'll simply search their rooms before the police do.'

'Evangeline!' It was one of the moments when her sheer nerve left me gasping. 'You can't! We can't! Suppose we got caught?'

'We will not get caught. You said yourself that Madame Defarge has disappeared—you can count on it that she'll lie low until after the police have come and gone. And Job is far too busy to have time to go back to his room this morning.'

'Unless he feels the need for a quick nip of blood to see him through the rigours of the script conference.'

'He needn't return for that—' Evangeline looked at me meaningfully. 'All he needs is a few moments in a quiet corner. Lora is still with him, his own private supply.'

'Oh!' She had me there. She knew I worried about poor Lora. Not that I really believed that Job might be—At least, in daylight I didn't. During these dark endless nights I could believe anything. And, come to think of it, I hadn't seen daylight—not proper daylight—since we'd been up here.

'Are you coming?' She was already opening the door.

'I suppose so.' She was going ahead, whether I accompanied her or not. Besides, I didn't want to miss anything. 'Two of us can work faster than one.'

It was just as well that I tapped on the door of Mrs Bright's room before Evangeline barged in.

'Who is it?' a choked voice called. We looked at each other. We had forgotten Alanna shared the room.

'Trixie,' I answered. 'And Evangeline. Are you all right? Can we come in?' Not that we wanted to now, but having knocked, we couldn't very well say, '*We'll come back when the room is empty.*'

'Of course!' We could hear swift footsteps cross the room, then the door was flung open and Alanna stood there, her eyes filled with tears.

'Are you all right?' I asked again. I could see Evangeline looking around impatiently, her fingers twitching to begin opening drawers and closets. She edged towards the fireplace while I spoke to Alanna.

'Yes, oh yes!' Alanna sighed rapturously. 'I'm just crying because I'm so happy. Look—!' She waved her left hand in front of my eyes and I was nearly blinded by the light dancing from the diamond. 'I'm engaged! To Barney! I've been dying to tell someone, but he says we must wait for a decent interval. So I can only wear the ring in the privacy of my own room. I slip upstairs every now and again, just to put it on—when Mother isn't around.'

'Congratulations. I mean, best wishes.' She needed them. Her mother was not going to take kindly to this development.

'Isn't it wonderful? I didn't know I could be so happy!'

In the background, Evangeline snorted.

161

'Yes, it's wonderful, dear. I'm very happy for you.' I spoke loudly to cover Evangeline's sound effects. She only sends congratulations for the divorce.

'Of course, I know my mother is going to be upset—' She lowered her voice, as though imparting a secret no one could have suspected. 'But Barney says she'll get used to the idea.'

In about a million years. 'Actually, we were looking for your mother.' I had to get us out of there. My own ability to rhapsodize over Love's Young Dream has diminished considerably over the years and Martha had just about worn it out.

'I haven't seen her lately,' Alanna assured us unnecessarily. If she had, the diamond would still be hidden on a chain around her neck, or wherever girls hid it these days.

'Then we must look elsewhere.' Evangeline swept forward and managed to give Alanna a brilliant smile. '*So* happy about your news, my dear, and don't worry—we'll keep it secret.'

Back in the hallway, with the door closed safely behind us, Evangeline vented her real feelings. 'Well, that was a washout!' She glared at me as though it had been my fault.

'Let's forget the whole thing,' I suggested, without any real hope. 'Maybe it just isn't our day.'

'It won't be if we don't find that evidence before the police do!' She was already moving purposefully towards Job's suite. At least she had learned enough of a lesson to knock this time.

There was silence from within. So why did the hairs begin to rise on the back of my neck?

'Evangeline,' I said uneasily, 'why don't we check downstairs first and make sure both Job and Lora are still in the canteen?'

'Nonsense!' But she gave in to my fears enough to knock a second time. There was still silence.

'You see? No one's in.' She opened the door and we stepped inside.

'Hello, girls.' Job looked up from the fridge. 'Happy Hour

162

already? What's the matter, you run out of brandy and you're settling for the weaker stuff?'

CHAPTER 18

Why do I let her talk me into these things? There was no Had-I-But-Known about it. I *knew* it was a crazy idea. I *knew* we should stay out of this and let the police handle it. I *knew* we shouldn't have gone out to search everybody's room. I *knew* we should never have opened that door . . .

'Cat got your tongues?' Job closed the fridge door and straightened up. I didn't like the way he grinned at us.

'Hey, relax! Lora told me she let you stash your white wine in my fridge. I don't mind. I think you might have asked *me*, but I don't really mind.'

'That's very kind of you,' Evangeline said weakly.

'I'm all heart.' He was still grinning. 'You girls must have noticed that by now.' His grin faded slowly. 'So, tell me, what else have you noticed?'

'Nothing!' I squeaked. 'Nothing at all!'

'So why don't I believe you? Could it be the way you've been looking at me lately? And avoiding me? Maybe Lora's been telling you things? That kid's got a great imagination. I may have made a mistake about her.'

If he hadn't, she was the first woman he'd never made a mistake about, but it didn't seem the right moment to point this out.

'Of course, her imagination isn't as great as yours, but she's young yet. Give her time and she'll be right up there on the broomstick with you. No reputation will be safe.' He sighed deeply, his shoulders drooped, he was a man betrayed. 'And I thought you were my friends.'

'We were . . . we *are!*' *Get me out of this and I'll never listen to Evangeline again*, I prayed silently. 'And Lora didn't tell us anything. Nothing at all! In fact, she was trying to shield you.'

'Shield me from what?' he asked softly.

163

'From . . . from . . .'

'It's no use, Job,' Evangeline said crisply. 'The game is up. You might as well confess.'

'Confess to what? This is worse than the nineteen-fifties—' He advanced upon us menacingly. 'Just what have I been accused of?'

'As though you didn't know!' Evangeline dodged around him and swooped on the fridge. She tore open its door and pointed inside dramatically. 'Deny that—Job Farraday, Vampire!'

His face went blank. He stared at Evangeline, at the fridge, at me. He began to twitch, then slumped to a sitting position on the floor, his whole body heaving and jerking. For a terrible moment, I thought we'd killed him.

'You crazy broads!' he wheezed. I realized he was laughing. 'You dumb crazy broads! You'd believe anything, wouldn't you?'

I began to get the awful feeling that we had made fools of ourselves.

'It's a good bluff, Job, but it won't work.' Evangeline was made of sterner stuff. 'How else can you explain—' she reached in the fridge and pulled out one of the bottles of blood—'*this*?'

'Don't drop it!' He scrambled to his feet; he wasn't laughing now. 'For Christ's sake, put that down! Carefully.'

'Evangeline,' I said, 'maybe you'd better.'

'Damn right, she'd better!' Job reached out for the bottle. 'We wouldn't want a nasty accident.'

'Don't you dare threaten me!' Evangeline backed away.

'Who's threatening? I just don't have any blood to spare. You drop that and I could die if anything happens to me.'

'Job—' Reminded of his hypochondria, I was beginning to suspect the truth. 'Job, whose blood is that, anyway?'

'Mine, of course. Whose did you think it—No!' He held up his hand. 'Don't tell me. I don't want to know. What the hell do you think I am? No, don't tell me that, either. I know. A vampire, right?'

164

Our silence answered him. He shook his head and gently replaced the blood in the fridge.

'Crazy, crazy broads,' he said. 'Don't you know everybody who knows anything travels with a supply of their own blood these days? If anything happens and we have to have an operation, you think we want to risk getting infected with AIDS? It's my own blood—from my own veins. And it's going *back* into my own veins if—God forbid—I have any kind of accident or need treatment. Even if I don't, I'll take it back the way athletes do—before an important match to give them that extra boost. Vampire, hell! You girls ought to get your heads examined!'

I hadn't known Evangeline could still blush, but she definitely went a deep pink. She avoided meeting my eyes.

'Maybe we ought to be going,' I suggested weakly.

'Maybe you ought,' Job agreed.

'I just hope you feel as silly as I do,' I fumed at Evangeline, back in our suite. I might have saved my breath, I could see she wasn't listening. She had that abstracted look on her face that I have grown to know and distrust. Furthermore, I didn't like the way she was looking at Griselda's door.

'No, Evangeline. No, no, no!' I moved to block her path.

'Just one little peek.' She evaded me easily—she gets so much practice—and had her hand on the doorknob before I could stop her.

'At least, knock,' I pleaded.

'There's no one there,' she said triumphantly.

'Well, it's the first time.' She didn't deserve such luck—and she didn't appreciate it. She sailed into the room as though it were her due.

Whatever else you might say about her, Griselda was tidy. The room had a Spartan cleanliness. Not an eyebrow pencil was out of place; not a shred of clothing was in sight.

'I don't believe it!' Evangeline took it as a personal insult. 'It's unnatural! I always said she wasn't a proper actress. No one can have a room like this without a dresser travelling with her.'

'Of course, she has Igor . . .' I suggested.

165

'Igor! That's it!' Evangeline whirled about. 'She wouldn't risk keeping anything incriminating in a place so close to *us*. Anything she doesn't want us to see will be upstairs in Igor's room.'

'But I thought we were suspecting Mrs Bright.' I couldn't see how Grisly had suddenly entered the picture, then I could. 'This is sheer nosiness, Evangeline, and you know it. Grisly and Igor have nothing to do with—'

'Haven't they?' Evangeline assumed that faraway look again. 'Igor spent a lot of time in Transylvania—vampire country! Perhaps he walks by night or flies!' She was almost flying across the room herself. 'I think we should search his room, if only to eliminate him. You know it would never occur to the police to suspect him.'

'Not for the reason you suspect him, anyway. I can just see how that would look on a police report: *Investigating suspected vampire. Searched room for* ... for what? Bat droppings?'

'You've got it, Trixie! That's exactly what we'll look for.'

'Oh, now, wait a minute—'

'Didn't you notice the way he looked at the bats? As though they were almost friends—*he* wasn't afraid of them. But shhh—' She opened the main door. 'It would not be wise to continue this conversation in the corridor. Just follow me ...'

It was against my better judgement, but somebody had to be around to pull her out of trouble when she got caught. I followed her down the hallway, past the back stairs the minions used to reach their quarters and round a hidden corner I had never realized was there.

'Oh!' We had startled Meta, who was leaning into an aperture in the wall and seemed to be rattling dishes.

'Just as I thought!' Evangeline approached and leaned over her shoulder, making her even more nervous. 'A dumb waiter! *That* was why you never minded carrying trays up to us—and why the food was always lukewarm when it arrived. You put it on the dumb waiter while you took the stairs and then retrieved it.'

'Well, I'm sorry.' Meta was immediately on the defen-

166

sive. 'I do the best I can, but it isn't easy without a proper staff.'

'And you *are* accustomed to a proper staff—or *were*.'

'Yes,' Meta sighed. 'Before the hotel closed down, we had a regular full-time staff and a core of part-timers we could call on in the height of the season.' She sighed again. 'Not that we ever had much of a season up here.'

'You *own* this hotel?' Now that I thought about it, I shouldn't have been so startled. Meta had always assumed too much responsibility for a mere minion. And I had noticed from the first that the catering had been too formal for location standards—it was more along the wedding reception line.

'The family does,' Meta said. 'But we'd pretty much given up on it. We'd just closed it down when Job's offer came along—and it was a godsend. My parents are looking for a new hotel somewhere down on the South Coast. We'll move down when this film-lease is over. Most of us will,' she corrected herself.

'But not Griff?' That was something else I should have noticed. Once you looked for it, the family resemblance was clear. 'He *is* your brother?'

'Yes,' she sighed. 'When your eye stops being distracted by all those silly costumes, you can spot it, can't you? He wasn't always like that, but he was fascinated by old films and it got worse as he grew older. I guess fantasy just runs in the family. My father isn't much better. Do you know what my real name is? Demeta! Demeta—how do you like that? I shortened it as soon as I could. How would *you* like to be named after a fictional ship? The good ship *Demeter* that carried Dracula to these shores!' She laughed wildly. 'Sometimes I think the whole area is cursed! Legends and superstitions are born in our very bones and we can't escape them!'

'Tell me, my dear—' Heedless of Meta's personal anguish, Evangeline had been concentrating on the dumb waiter. 'How far up does this go? Is the machinery for it in the basement or the roof?'

'The housing is up in the loft.' Bewildered by the change of subject, Meta responded automatically. 'Why?'

167

'And the dumb waiter goes all the way up there? Completely? So that anyone crouched inside it could step out into the loft, disturb the bats, and go down again without ever having to use the stairs?'

'The bats!' Meta laughed again, on the verge of hysteria. It was obvious that we weren't going to get a great deal more out of her. 'That was the last straw! Sometimes I think the best thing that could happen would be if the whole damned building burned to the ground! Yes, and *Yesterday's Dreams*, too. Then we could collect the insurance and leave for ever!'

'No, Evangeline,' I said. 'No, no, no!'

'I was merely thinking, Trixie, that it would not be necessary to crouch inside the dumb waiter. One could stand on top of it and hoist oneself to the loft level from just above the top floor.'

'Speak for yourself. *This* one couldn't.'

'Perhaps not, but someone who had been working as a tumbler and acrobat could. Without any difficulty. And someone who was not afraid of bats would have no difficulty in moving among them, opening the trapdoor to the hallway below and driving them down through it to terrorize the minions.'

'Why should he want to do that?'

'I don't know, but it proves that it's more important than ever that we search Igor's room.'

I had to hand it to her, she could twist anything to her own advantage—and she might even have a point there. Taking a quick look into Igor's room no longer seemed like such a screwy notion. Of course, I still didn't believe that he was a vampire, or anything like that, but . . .

Igor's room was a mess! There was more than the normal untidiness of the unattached male, there was a strange tattiness about the place. Looking more closely, I saw tiny snippets of coloured threads everywhere—on the upholstery, the carpet, and even the bed.

'What on earth—?' Evangeline stared incredulously at multicoloured lint and gold fluff lying over everything like exotic dust. Two chairs were placed companionably on either side of a round table holding a lighted lamp, two pairs of reading glasses and two pairs of scissors. 'All that's missing here is the dressmaker's dummy.'

'Ye-es, but . . .' It looked cosy, domestic, intimate—and as though the occupants of the room had just stepped outside for a minute and would soon be back. Something else bothered me about the scene. Was it something Evangeline had said?

'Evangeline—' I looked around uneasily. 'Let's get out of here.'

'Patience, Trixie, patience. We just got here.' She opened the closet door, but what she saw—rather, what she didn't see—disappointed her.

'Nothing!' She backed out frowning. 'But there *must* be something here. I can *feel* it.'

'Maybe there was, but it's gone now.' I looked pointedly at the cheerful blaze crackling away behind the firescreen. It was brighter, warmer and more orderly than any fire we had been able to make. Igor had obviously learned more than supernatural secrets on his Transylvanian travels.

'That's only too possible.' Evangeline crossed to the fire, picked up the poker, leaned over the firescreen and sniffed. 'Do you smell something strange?'

'No-o-o . . . Maybe . . .' I inhaled deeply and a peculiar scent caught at my sinuses. 'Yes. Yes, I think I do.'

'I knew it!' She shoved aside the firescreen and began poking vigorously at the fire, sending a shower of sparks up the chimney. 'They've been destroying the evidence!'

'Evangeline, be careful!' She was really attacking the fire now. Chunks of blazing wood tumbled from the grate to fall into the embers on the hearth. 'You're tearing that fire apart. They'll know someone's been in here.'

'Nonsense! These fires always collapse into the embers when they die. They'll never notice.'

'Girsly might not, but Igor knows a lot more about fires than we do.'

'Igor knows a lot more about a lot of things.' Evangeline gave up on the fire, having beaten it into flickering splinters of charred wood. I could see no trace of burned clothing in the ashes.

Neither could Evangeline. She glared at the fireplace and threw down the poker in disgust. I didn't bother to protest, not even when she went over to the dresser and began pulling out drawers. There was no way we were going to be able to cover our tracks—all we could do was get out before we were caught in the act and hope that the police would be blamed for the shambles.

And it was a shambles. The closet door stood ajar; ashes spilled across the hearthstone; and even now Evangeline was not shutting the drawers properly after rummaging through them.

'There *must* be something.' Evangeline spoke between clenched teeth. 'You can see they've been cutting up the bloodstained clothing.'

We looked again at the two chairs beside the table with the lamp glowing down on the companionable pairs of scissors and reading glasses. Somehow, the scene didn't look as sinister as Evangeline seemed to think. There was something almost serene about it.

Behind the table, in the shadows against the far wall, was a large theatrical travelling trunk—the kind they don't make any more. Battered and well-used, it came from the pre-war era of travel on the grand scale, plastered with labels from defunct shipping lines, obsolete railways and the formerly Grand Hotels of several continents.

Just looking at it brought on a case of acute nostalgia. It was so familiar, so much a part of all our pasts. Of course, most of the stickers weren't even in English, but the pictorial representations of palatial destinations and the names of bomb-razed theatres in long-dead cities were familiar in any language. Griff would have sold his soul for that trunk.

'You're right, Trixie.' Evangeline had followed my gaze. 'We haven't checked the trunk.' She started towards it.

'But—' My protest died on my lips as I suddenly realized what I was seeing: dangling from under a corner of the lid was a fragment of white satin ribbon.

As though hypnotized, I went over and tugged at it

170

gently. Weakened by decades of constant use, the lid was no longer so tight-fitting; it disgorged more of the ribbon, now aged into a soft cream colour, but unmistakable. I stared at it unbelievingly.

'What is it?' Evangeline, too, stared at the length of ribbon. 'Do you see any bloodspots on it?'

'No. No, it's not that. It's just—' I tugged at the ribbon again, but the lid had disgorged as much as it was going to. The ribbon was attached to something heavier which had clunked against the lid and was holding fast.

'It's the ribbon from my old dancing shoes! I'm sure it is!'

'Help me get this open!' Evangeline pushed at the lid. She didn't ask how I knew, or doubt that I did. We all have a sixth sense about old belongings that have almost been a part of us.

'Maybe if we had a nail file . . .' When I played the chorus girl who was in love with an FBI undercover man, we had opened a whole safe with nothing more than my nail file and found the gangster's secret set of accounts detailing payments for murder jobs and sent him to the electric chair.

'Try the scissors.' Evangeline snatched the smaller pair from the table and jabbed the points into the lock.

Nothing happened.

'Hit it! That worked in *A Bullet from the Bride*.' I no longer had any qualms about breaking into Igor's trunk. The satin ribbon hung from beneath the lid like a long mocking tongue. I doubled up my fist and thumped at the lock.

'Ouch!'

'Try the poker,' Evangeline said, twisting the scissors in the lock.

I turned to get the poker—and froze. We had been so absorbed in what we were doing, we hadn't heard the door open behind us.

'Dear ladies, are you having difficulties?' Igor stood in the doorway, smiling sardonically at us.

'Did I neglect to leave the key in the lock? How remiss of me!'

171

CHAPTER 19

'Call the police!' Grisly was behind, seething with righteous indignation. 'Have them arrested! They are thieves! Meddlers! Call the police at once!'

'Hush, beloved.' Igor pulled her into the room and patted her shoulder. 'They are stealing nothing and it is not yet a criminal offence to be a meddler.' He closed the door firmly. 'There is no need for the police to be involved. We will handle this ourselves.'

'You are too soft!' Griselda spat, straight out of *Night of the Quislings*.

'This is obviously a case of people living in glass houses not wishing to throw stones, Trixie,' Evangeline said. 'I don't believe they want to have anything to do with the police themselves.'

'You are right,' Igor admitted. 'I have had enough of the Gestapo, the police, the officials, in my lifetime. I no longer trust even the best of them—if there *is* a best! Permit me—' Deftly, he removed the scissors from Evangeline's hand.

I was glad I hadn't had time to reach the poker. I didn't look quite so silly, I hoped.

'Those *are* my dancing shoes!' Attack was the best defence. 'The ones stolen from *Yesterday's Dreams*. I suppose you stole the costumes, too. But why?'

'I had my reasons.' Igor's smile was not ingratiating, but I didn't like it any better.

'Such as?' Evangeline challenged.

'Sentiment?' Igor offered. 'Memories?' He shrugged. 'Believe what you will.'

'I'd rather know the truth.'

'But what is truth? The eternal question of the philosopher.'

'Do not waste your breath with them!' Griselda moved restlessly, looking everywhere except at us—and at the fireplace. 'Throw them out!'

'Not yet, my love. First, we must find out what they have discovered.'

'I've discovered my dancing shoes, for one thing!' I was not going to let Igor keep straying from the point.

'Ah yes, that upsets you. Allow me—' He went over to the trunk, took a small key from his pocket, inserted it in the lock and lifted back the lid. A strong scent of attar of roses and exotic spices eddied out from it—the scent we thought had been coming from burning cloth in the fireplace.

'Allow me to return them to you.' He held out the shoes to me, dangling from their ribbons. 'Although, technically, I believe they belong to our friend Griff.'

'I'll see that he gets them back.' I clutched the shoes to me, ridiculously happy to have them in my possession again, however briefly.

'Aha!' Evangeline had taken advantage of our little interlude to dive into the trunk. She surfaced clutching the gipsy jacket of Griselda's old costume. 'This also belongs to Griff, I believe.' She held it by the shoulders and shook it out. 'But what have you been doing to it?'

Well might she ask. The hems drooped loosely, sprouting threads. Darker streaks of colour showed where the material had once been doubled over and stitched into place. The cloth-covered buttons were missing and forlorn threads drooped opposite the buttonholes.

'Nossing!' Griselda said quickly. 'Ve do nossing!' Her accent was so thick, she practically needed an interpreter. She'd been up to something all right.

'You've cut all the threads to let down the hems.' Evangeline looked from the jacket to the scissors on the table. 'Now if you'd been letting out the *seams*, I might understand. Although—' her gaze swept Griselda's waist, she'd been waiting a long time to get her own back on *that* score— 'I doubt that there was enough material in the gussets to alter it to fit your present size.'

'Nossing!' Griselda sent one panic-stricken glance—it was her mistake—towards the chimney before turning back to glare hatred at Evangeline. 'I tell you, ve do nossing!'

173

Tell it to the Marines! I edged over in the direction of the fireplace and picked up the poker while Grisly and Evangeline were still confronting each other. Igor was standing back, watching us all with interest. I had the feeling that he knew what I was doing, but had decided not to interfere.

'Bats!' I squealed, thrusting the poker up the chimney and churning about with it. 'I'm sure I heard a bat up there!'

'Vot are you doing? Stop that!' Grisly started towards me, but it was too late.

A chain of bright gleaming metal slithered down the chimney, bringing a shower of soot with it. It was followed by another, and another, until finally, a heap of gold glittered in the soot and ashes on the hearthstone.

'It iss not vot you think!' Griselda gasped. Now that she had been discovered, her accent was returning to normal.

Since we were both too stunned to think at all, Evangeline and I stood there with expressions so blank they passed for disbelief.

'Perhaps we should explain, my love,' Igor said.

'To *them?*' Griselda's lip curled.

They are the ones who have discovered our secret. We must earn their silence. Please—' He gestured to us. 'Sit down.'

Griselda was the first to do so. She took one of the chairs beside the table, sitting bolt upright, as imperious as when she had played *The Empress of All the Russias*.

I had expected Igor to take the consort's chair opposite her. Instead, he sank to the ground at her feet—the jester's position—leaning his head against her knee, totally relaxed and smiling at us.

'Please—' he invited again, stretching out his arm and lazily tugging at the jacket still in Evangeline's grasp.

'Thank you, I prefer to stand,' Evangeline said coldly. She let the jacket slip through her fingers reluctantly, still eyeing it as though hoping to discover at least one bloodstain. But we had travelled a long way beyond our original suspicions.

'I prefer to stand, too,' I said. *Preferably near the door.*

'It vass a long time ago—' Clearly, Griselda regretted sitting down herself. The performer who was standing always commanded the scene, but she was trying her best. 'Und life vass very different—'

'Half of Europe was Nazi-occupied and it was just a matter of time for the other half.' Evangeline took the cue and ran with it; she wasn't going to let Griselda take control of this scene. 'You weren't the first people to convert everything into gold and sew the gold into your clothing.'

'And then lose the gold as you escaped.' I was right there with her. At our ages, there was nothing new under the sun. We had seen—or heard—it all before.

'Then,' Igor said, 'you can understand why we felt that our friend Griff, worthy though he is, was in possession of more than his due. He may have bought our costumes, but—' With a fingernail, Igor slit the last remaining stitches on some gold braid and flicked out a short length of gold chain with the agility of a conjuror.

'Ve could not believe it, seeing our costumes again in *Yesterday's Dreams!* Und when our fingers told us that the chains were still in place, ve had to make sure that they were still the right ones, that no one had switched them over the years . . .' Griselda captured the chain and coiled it neatly on the table beside her.

'And so you kept Griff at your side all day,' Evangeline said. 'While Igor went down to the town and burgled the exhibition.'

'Griff had no right to the gold ve sacrificed to save!'

'Naturally, we will see that the costumes are restored to him,' Igor said. 'But we see no reason to allow him to keep something that he never knew he had—and to which he can surely have no claim.'

'You vill not betray us?' It started as a command; it ended as a plea.

'Of course not!' It burst from me spontaneously, then I looked at Evangeline. We all looked at Evangeline.

175

'No-o-o . . .' She sounded as though the decision was against her better judgement, then rallied. 'I quite understand. Those of us—' She glared at me, defying me to contradict her. 'Those of us in . . . late middle age . . . must consider our futures.'

'I'll go along with that,' I said. 'No one could criticize you for retrieving your own property. Griff has no claim to it at all.'

'Wait a minute.' Evangeline had thought of a criticism. 'What about that knife in my back? In my replica's back?'

'Ah!' Igor shrugged. 'A little joke of my lady's. You did not take it amiss?'

'And what about the Padfoot?' Evangeline was remembering our desperate race for life. 'Was that another joke of your lady's?'

'Padfoot?' I could see that Igor was genuinely puzzled. 'A joke, perhaps, but not one of ours.'

Griselda started to open her mouth and Igor leaned heavily on her foot. She closed her mouth again, but her eyes were thoughtful.

'Now that you've found each other again, as well as your youthful nest egg—' I didn't want to sound sentimental, but it was as good a way as any of changing a dangerous subject—'you *are* going to stay together, aren't you?'

Igor turned his head abruptly, so that his face was half hidden against Griselda's skirt. His body went still. He waited.

'Much has been given back to us . . .' Griselda said slowly. Her hand slid down to tousle Igor's hair. 'It would be churlish to turn our backs on it.'

Igor's body relaxed. A deep heart-rending dimple appeared in his cheek. With the worse side of his profile buried in Griselda's skirt, he looked almost as he must have looked when he was the matinee idol of Budapest. One hand crept up to capture Griselda's hand and bring it down to his lips.

My vision blurred with a sudden mist. Maybe she didn't deserve it, but Grisly was strolling off into the sunset with the love of her life.

176

Evangeline snorted. It was sheer jealousy, but it called us back to the present moment.

'That's all very well,' she said. 'But the police are still going to arrive at any moment and begin searching the house. They're quite likely to impound any gold they find lying around—and it could be years before you prove ownership and get it back.'

'The chimney!' Griselda sprang to her feet. Igor's head clunked against the chair leg. 'Ve must replace der gold in der chimney!'

'You're right!' And I had been the one to disturb the safe hiding-place. Guilt swept over me. I dived for the hearth, scrabbling for the gold chains, heedless of the soot staining my hands.

Griselda crouched beside me, the large pigeon's blood ruby on her finger glinting in the weak flame that suddenly broke from a charred piece of wood. I had never seen the ring before, nor the matching stud earrings she was wearing.

'I suppose the jewels were sewn under the cloth of the buttons.' Evangeline had not missed the deep ruby gleam either.

Griselda nodded, too intent on taking the chains from me and returning them to their hiding nook inside the chimney to comment on Evangeline's cleverness. The already-loosened soot rained down on us.

'You're both getting filthy!' Evangeline was piqued. 'You'll need a bath before you're fit for civilized society again.'

'Since present company is always excepted—' I was getting annoyed myself. 'We have plenty of time.'

'Time!' Igor looked at his watch. 'I am due on the set! We are shooting the Church Stairs sequence this afternoon.'

'No!' Griselda hurled herself at Igor from her crouching position, nearly knocking him over. 'No, it iss too dangerous! You are not to do this! Not when ve have just found each other again.'

'But who else can do it, my love? Old Igor has the knowledge, the experience, the agility . . . and there is no other stuntman available.'

177

'Stunt?' My blood ran cold. 'Igor, you *haven't* let Job talk you into that crazy fall down the Church Stairs?' But he had; Griselda's white face and desperate eyes told me so.

'Calm yourself, little one. It is not so frightening. There is a framework constructed within the costume that will allow me to soar like a bird—or a bat.' He gave me an impish grin. 'And, if the apparatus does not deliver all that Job expects—well, I am the best tumbler in the Carpathians and I have learned many tricks from circus acrobats. It is safer for me to do this stunt than it would be for anyone else.'

'Please, Igor!' Griselda clung to him, as unconvinced as I was. 'Do not do this, I beg you—'

'There's always been a pretty high mortality rate among stuntmen on Job's films,' I pointed out grimly. 'You'd better listen to her.'

'Then I will delay long enough to change the beneficiary on my insurance form.' Igor held Griselda close for a moment. 'But do not fear that you will collect it. I will come back to you.'

'If you do not, I vill kill Job,' Griselda vowed. 'Maybe I kill him anyway.'

She meant it and I didn't blame her. Job had crossed so many people over the years it was a wonder to everyone that he was still alive.

'I am coming with you,' Griselda said.

'We are all coming with you,' Evangeline corrected.

'Of course.' Igor looked at us with amusement. 'But first, I think, you must clean yourselves so that you no longer resemble chimney sweeps. One would not wish the police to have their attention directed to the chimneys. I will go and get into my costume and see you at the Church Stairs.'

We hurried as fast as we could, but soot has a way of sinking into the pores and it took longer than we intended. Also, three women trying to share the same bathroom didn't expedite matters.

By the time we arrived at the Church Stairs, the Unit was assembled and ready to begin shooting. The usual cluster of minions surrounded the small hunched figure behind the pedlar's tray.

I saw Evangeline frown and knew that her initial reaction was the same as mine: Igor was overdoing it. We were not at all hunched. Good carriage is part of our stock-in-trade and, when you're as short as I am, you're always standing as tall as you can, reaching for that extra inch or so. Of course, Igor was hunched anyway, but I was sure I'd seen him standing taller than that.

As we watched, the minor minions moved away, leaving Igor deep in concentrated debate with Hobie, Barney and Job. I didn't like the way Barney held his head cocked sceptically to one side. And there was something about the way Igor was moving . . .

'Good God!' Evangeline said. 'I believe they've got him on a skateboard!'

Griselda moaned in terror. I felt like moaning myself.

'This is not going to work! This is never going to work!' Evangeline was doing nothing for poor Grisly's morale, nor mine either. 'We've got to stop them!'

'How?' Already Job was moving back to stand with Koji at the principal camera. Barney was fumbling with a wire attached to the leg of the pedlar's table-tray. I remembered that it was due to go flying through the air. So was Igor.

Hobie seemed to be giving last-minute instructions to Igor, emphasizing some vital point with gestures that looked more confusing than clarifying.

'Don't let them do this!' Griselda was clutching at Evangeline's arm. 'You are strong. You can stop them.'

'LIGHTS! . . . CAMERA! . . . ACTION!'

As the familiar commands rang out, Evangeline hesitated. We all did. The discipline had been so deeply ingrained in us that we couldn't help it.

The clapperboard sounded and Igor glided forward, arms extending slowly to balance himself and lock the glider frame into place beneath the batwing sleeves. I wondered whether he was doubling for Evangeline or me.

The skateboard gathered speed as it rolled down the slight incline to the top of the steps, but Igor seemed to be

179

in control of it. Head bent, watching the ground as he neared the top step, he adjusted his balance and began to swing his arms upward, preparatory to flight.

Then he raised his head, making a final assessment of the pitch of the steps, the distance to the first landing-stage, the complete distance to the safety of level ground so far below. He needed all his skills now.

Abruptly, his body tensed and the skateboard swerved erratically.

We saw it, too: Dracula stood motionless at the bottom of the stairs, looking up expectantly.

Igor gave a thin high-pitched cry as he tilted over the edge of the top step; his arms swung wildly as he tried to activate the mechanism inside the costume. He might have succeeded if so much of his attention had not been riveted on that menacing figure below.

Dracula waited there to claim his own. Fabian de Bourne in full costume—But it couldn't be! Fabian was dead!

Igor crashed down to the first landing, lurched across it and pitched down the second set of steps. He seemed to be trying to kick himself free of the skateboard, but the long skirts impeded him. He swayed precariously, then fell head-long down the next flight.

The minions were screaming, Barney was swearing, Hobie was frozen in horror. Koji kept the camera recording—that man would film the end of the world and never worry about whether there'd be anybody left to view it.

'Igor!' Griselda screamed. 'Igor!'

Dracula took the steps two at a time, racing up to the huddled body. There was something almost recognizable about the way he moved. He bent over the body—and I had seen that movement before, too.

'Des!' I cried thankfully. 'It's Des!'

The minions began swarming down the stairs. Koji remained at his post. Job strode to the top of the stairs and stood there like a brooding menace surveying the scene below.

'Igor—' Griselda swayed at the top of the steps, in danger of falling herself. 'My Igor—'

'Yes, my love?' The blurred voice spoke from somewhere behind us. 'What is it?'

We whirled around. Gwenda was right behind us and for a moment I thought she was playing a cruel joke. Then she shifted position slightly and I saw that she was supporting a wan and unsteady Igor.

'Igor! Igor!' Griselda flung herself at him.

'Cwumbs, Twixie, I'm glad to see you!' Gwenda stepped back, allowing Griselda full possession of Igor. 'I found him lying in the corner beside the dumb waiter. At first, I thought he was dead. Then, when I brought him round and helped him up, he started muttering about the Gestapo and saying they could beat him to death before he'd talk. I thought he'd gone out of his mind. Oh, Twixie, I've been so fwightened!'

'He seems to be all right now.' Igor was embracing Griselda enthusiastically. 'It must have been just a temporary disorientation.' The shock of the attack had obviously spun his mind back to the nightmare time when unexpected blows and beatings had been a way of life. Having survived that, a mere tap in the head was not going to put him out of action for long now.

'Oh, but, Twixie, *somebody* knocked him out. It couldn't have been the Gestapo, but who—'

'Someone who wanted to take his place in the scene.' Evangeline looked down the long length of the Church Stairs. 'Someone who thought it would further her career, or cement her relationship with her lover . . .'

Barney was delicately untangling the voluminous black skirts that had wrapped around her body shrouding her head. We looked down on the pale bloodless face of Lora.

We hadn't believed Job when he intimated that she was a scheming manipulative liar. At least, I hadn't.

Evangeline walked over to stand beside Job, who was still gazing down impassively at the scene below.

In the distance a siren wailed. *Now* the police were arriving, probably alerted by a telephone call from one of the minions. I hoped there was an ambulance on the way, too, but I didn't know whether I hoped it would arrive in time or not. If it wasn't already too late.

'Something went wrong,' Hobie wailed. 'The struts didn't hold. And the skateboard should have slipped free before the first tumble.'

'It was a lousy idea, anyway.' Job shrugged. 'You win some, you lose some.'

CHAPTER 20

'It wasn't your fault, Des.' I tried to comfort him. 'Stop blaming yourself.'

The police had come and gone—but they would be back. Meanwhile, the minions had scattered. Gwenda, Meta and Griselda had accompanied Igor to the hospital to make sure that his concussion was not serious. Evangeline and I were trying to convince poor Des that he was blameless.

'But if I hadn't been showing off . . .' Des wouldn't stop agonizing. 'I thought coming up here in full make-up would show everyone that I could double in any missing shots—close-ups included. I even studied pictures of Fabian and deliberately used the same make-up—' He broke off, shuddering.

'It wasn't your fault.' Evangeline took up the refrain, refilling the glass of brandy in his shaking hand.

'But I tried so hard to look just like Fabian. Deliberately. If I hadn't—' He gulped the brandy, his eyes haunted.

'It was when she looked down and saw me—' He could not stop replaying the scene in his mind. 'That was when she lost her balance—*why* she lost her balance. If I hadn't been made up as Fabian—It was all my fault! I was responsible—'

'Just remember, kid—if she hadn't killed Fabian in the first place, it wouldn't have bothered her to see you standing there looking just like him.' Job walked over and helped himself to brandy from the decanter we had brought downstairs with us. Uninvited, of course. Neither Evangeline nor

182

I had spoken to him since his heartless remark at the scene of Lora's death.

'You girls are still mad at me, aren't you?'

We ignored him. Pointedly. We were sitting here in the Jet Shop set because both of us had been so furious with Job over his callous dismissal of his young mistress's life that we had refused to set foot over his threshold. Nor would we allow him into our suite. The Jet Shop was the nearest thing to neutral territory on which to meet. Not that we wanted to meet him, but he was still the Director.

'But why should Lora kill Fabian?' Des was anxious for any sort of explanation that would ease his conscience.

'Why not?' Job wasn't going to keep out of the conversation. 'She hated Fabian for ditching her. I guess she hated me, too.' He shrugged. 'That's all the thanks you get for picking somebody up off the floor and dusting off the pieces.'

'You mean *Lora* was the American girlfriend Fabian jilted?' I forgot I wasn't speaking to Job. Suddenly it all began to make sense.

'The girl Madame Defarge lied about, undermined, and tricked out of Alanna's way!' Evangeline's eyes gleamed. 'No wonder Lora used *her* knitting needle, then planted it back in the knitting-bag to try to pin the murder on her.'

'Poor Lora.' I found I could still feel sorry for the girl. 'She'd been given a pretty raw deal all around.'

'Poor Lora, my left hind foot!' Evangeline exploded. ('*You* said it,' Job muttered.) '*She* must have been the one who chased us with that car rigged up as the Padfoot. She was trying to kill *us*, too!'

'I don't think so,' Job said. 'I think she just wanted to louse up the filming . . . at first. You girls are pretty tough—and everybody knows it. She wasn't risking much giving you two a workout. At worst, you'd just be out of action a couple of days, recovering.'

'But if we hadn't realized it was a car—' Evangeline was so incensed, she forgot she'd sent Job to Coventry and addressed him directly. 'If we'd come back here claiming we'd been chased by the Padfoot, people would have thought we'd gone mad. And no doubt the dear girl would have encouraged that notion for all she was worth—which wasn't much!'

'Naw, she'd probably have been sympathetic and agreed with you. Like the way she kept everybody all upset over the bats. Maybe it was just a dry run with you two to get the rumour going, then she'd have used the Padfoot rig again to give Fabian a good scare. Or maybe kill him.' Job shook his head. 'But, like Trixie says, the poor kid got a rough deal. It was that Fabian. I blame him for everything.'

'Then why did you hire him for this picture, if you felt that way about him?' I was genuinely curious. Job's thought processes had always been a matter for great speculation among his colleagues.

'I dunno.' Job was evasive. 'Maybe I thought it would help Lora get over him if she saw him in action. He wasn't exactly a lovable character when he got the bit in his teeth in a work situation.'

Evangeline snorted. Job spoke as though *he* was!

'So OK,' he admitted. 'Maybe I also thought I could give him a rough time. Maybe I thought it would make Lora feel better if she could see him sweat.'

'Oh, Job . . .' I sighed.

'Yeah, I know.' He swung around to stare into the fire, his back to us. 'It just didn't work out that way. I guess I shoulda kept them apart.'

'I suppose she *was* naked when she killed him.' Evangeline twisted the knife. 'Fabian wouldn't have been suspicious about a tryst with *her*. He'd have assumed she was crazy enough about him to come back to him on any terms and take up where they left off.'

'His ego was big enough,' Job agreed. 'And maybe he was right. She sure wasn't crazy about me—even though she put on a good act.'

'Poor Lora.' I sighed again. She certainly couldn't pick her men. First Fabian, then Job. It was a wonder Lora had been able to pass for sane at all.

'I suppose she actually was a bit mad.' Des was cheering up.

'Mad as a hatter.' Evangeline brooded into the fire. 'She had to be, to engineer those bat incidents. I knew that Igor, with his circus training, could have ridden up to the loft on top on the dumb waiter; I should have realized that a slim athletic young woman was also capable of it.'

'Do you think one of the bats really bit her when she was disturbing them?' I knew that she had kept the wound open by constantly clawing at it and calling attention to it. 'Or did she puncture her own neck with the tip of the knitting needle?'

'I think she did it herself,' Job said. 'She told me she had a great idea for getting us together so that it would look innocent—'

Evangeline snorted.

'Yeah, well, everybody hasn't got your kind of mind.'

'So Lora already had a knitting needle in her possession.' I jumped in quickly before Evangeline could reply. Her eyes narrowed as she watched the flickering flames.

'I guess she stole one from Ma Bright as soon as Bright came on the scene. God knows, that woman carried around enough needles to equip an army.'

'And then Lora planted the needle, coated with Fabian's blood, back in the knitting-bag. She even slipped it into the stitches from another needle on the very scarf being knitted for Fabian. That would have made Madame Defarge the Number One Suspect all right. And she realized it when she saw that knitting needle. So she ran away.' I decided not to mention that she had first replanted the evidence on me.

'Yeah, and she hasn't come back yet.' Job spoke with the air of someone discovering a silver lining. 'Maybe she's left the country.' The dark cloud descended again. 'Too bad Lora didn't take that way out.'

'I believe she honestly thought she could get away with it,' Evangeline said. 'Right up to the minute when she looked down and saw—' Evangeline glanced at Des and broke off.

And saw Dracula waiting for her. And, for a disorientated moment, thought that a retribution beyond the human was upon her.

'She went over the edge—in more ways than one.' Leave it to Job!

'You have a touching line in epitaphs,' Evangeline said coldly.

'You have to feel sorry for her.' Des had come to a conclusion. 'But you're right, it wasn't my fault. It was all in her mind. I just happened to be there.'

'That's the way to look at it,' I approved. 'You weren't at all responsible for what happened.'

'I wouldn't like to think so. I feel awful enough already, bringing so much bad news. I'd hate to feel I was a Jonah all around.'

'What?' Evangeline snapped to attention. 'What bad news?'

'Oh—' Des looked confused. 'That's right. There was so much excitement, I forgot to tell you. Jasper has sold the house.'

'The house in St John's Wood?' Job obviously welcomed the change of subject.

'To a developer who's going to turn it into a block of luxury flats. We all have to get out. Maybe you two can move back in again when he's finished, but the rest of us will never be able to afford the rents. That's why I was so pleased about this job—I'm going to need all the money I can get. It was so kind of you to think of me, Trixie—'

'Never mind that.' I cut off his gratitude before Job got the idea that he could have hired him for an even lower salary. 'What's the rest of the bad news?' The way he'd been speaking, there had to be more.

Evangeline tensed.

'Well . . .' Sure enough, there was. 'The announcement was in *The Stage* this week. I suppose you haven't seen it up here?' He looked uncomfortable.

'Go on.' Evangeline was gritting her teeth.

'*Arsenic and Old Lace* is premiering at the Theatre Royal in Brighton next month, prior to a West End opening.' He

186

took a deep breath and plunged on. 'Starring Dame Cecile Savoy and Matilda Jordan.'

There was a long deafening silence, then Job began to laugh.

'That's one in the eye for you girls,' he whooped. 'Pipped at the post, eh? Now what are you going to do?' He wheezed and spluttered; he was having a great time. 'Tell you what, maybe we should do a sequel to this picture!'

He was so busy laughing he didn't see the deadly glint that had appeared in Evangeline's eyes.

'Hey, that's not such a bad idea!' he began to decide. We can stay up here another few weeks and shoot back-to-back.'

'But it's so cold up here, Job dear.' Evangeline's voice was so sweet it made my hair curl. Even Job looked momentarily mistrustful. 'It's freezing. In fact, I'm freezing right now. We need more coal on the fire.'

She advanced upon the fire. I couldn't see what she had in her hands—but I could guess.

'Hey!' Job watched her with growing alarm. 'What have you got there? What do you think you're doing?'

She let her actions speak for her.

'Stop that!' he howled as the first piece of jet hit the flames. 'Do you know how much those things cost?'

Of course she did. That was why she was doing it.

'Cut it out! Quit it!' He dropped to his knees and tried to pull one of the bigger pieces out of the fire. Failing that, he tried to catch other pieces as Evangeline threw them. But she was too fast for him, moving like a whirlwind around the room, hurling jet objects from every direction.

'Stop her!' He appealed to me. 'Make her stop!'

'But I'm cold, too, Job.' I picked up an ornately-carved bracelet and weighed it thoughtfully. Evangeline was doing a great job. They wouldn't be able to reconstruct this set again in a hurry.

'Don't you start!' He glared frantically at me, then turned to Des. 'Make them stop! They're out of control! They're crazy! Oow!' A large jet-backed hand mirror bounced off his skull on the way into the fire.

187

'Des, dear—' Evangeline sent him a vague smile. 'I'm afraid I'm about to have one of my ghastly headaches. Could you be an angel and run and get me some aspirin?' Des ran.

'No, girls, no!' Left alone, Job tried pleading again, still scrabbling to field the jet pieces as Evangeline hurled them.

I watched him for another minute, then strolled over and tossed the jet bracelet past him into the flames. Evangeline hadn't reached the mantelpiece yet, so I cleared that for her.

'No! No!' Job struggled to contain jet missiles coming from two directions now. 'What the hell do you think you're doing?'

'I think of it,' I said, 'as building a funeral pyre for Lora.'

'I don't know,' I said slowly, back in our suite. 'For a while there, back when we didn't show up in that mirror . . . for a crazy moment, I thought we might really be vampires. And for an even crazier moment, I thought it might not be so bad. At least we'd be immortal.'

'We already *are* immortal!' Evangeline threw back her head and stared into middle distance. 'We'll live for ever up there on the Silver Screen. Whatever happens to us, our captured images—our shadows—will go on and on . . . delighting audiences still unborn. We're the first generation of actors who have ever had that privilege given to us.'

'Maybe so . . .' Sometimes it seemed a doubtful privilege. 'And maybe we should have been more careful about what we let ourselves be captured in. We've both appeared in some clinkers. Even this idiocy about vampires—'

'Careful, Trixie.' She cut me off. 'We shouldn't bite the hands that have fed us all these years. We could only appear in what we were offered. We shouldn't mock our own achievements.'

'Not even vampire films?'

'Go *very* carefully, Trixie.' She looked thoughtful. 'I shall always remember dear Hamilton Dean in his appearances as Van Helsing in the original play of *Dracula*. At the very end, after his gracious curtain speech, as the audience were gathering up their wraps to go out into the night, he would turn back to them and say:

'Just one word of warning, ladies and gentlemen . . . There *are* such things!'